A Pixie's
Transformation

By Faith D. Eilertson

Illustrated by Kari Vick

This is a work of fiction. Names, characters, places, and incidents are either the products of the author's imagination or are used in a fictitious manner, and any resemblance to actual persons, living or dead, businesses, events, or locales is purely coincidental.

Edited by Sara Ensey
Cover and chapter illustrations by Kari Vick
Illustrations on pages 9, 60, 75 and 201 by Sandy Gramse

ISBN 13: 978-1-64343-910-5
Library of Congress Catalog Number: 2019906159
Printed in the United States of America
First Printing: 2022
26   25   24   23   22   5   4   3   2   1

Book design and typesetting by Tina Brackins
This book is typeset in Caslon Book and Luminari fonts.

Beaver's Pond Press
939 Seventh Street West
Saint Paul, MN 55102
(952) 829-8818
www.BeaversPondPress.com

Contact Faith D. Eilertson at www.faithdeilertson.com for school visits, book club discussions, and interviews.

To my husband, Scott, to whom I am
deeply indebted for his continual love,
encouragement, and support
as I authored this book.

1.

A New Home– New Mysteries

"Now you stay there where I can find you; if I need you, I'll be sure to clap the code. I'll bring you over to the new home soon, when I think it is safest to do so." And with that, Mrs. Gunderson closed her closet doors quietly while looking back to make certain that no other set of eyes had witnessed her conversation. Content to be a working suburban mother, she was very skilled at keeping the secret she had hidden for years in her closet. Even her own kids were kept away from this secret with Mr. Gunderson's help, despite knowing that it would answer a lot of questions the children had asked over the years. For example, how was it that during the school year their mother could correct all those classroom papers every day and still have so much extra time to relax and read the newspaper? Mrs. Gunderson's teacher friends always complained that there were never enough hours in the day to get their work done while keeping up with the housework and family life, but Mrs. Gunderson managed this all too well. Evelyn and Reed rarely witnessed their mother dusting or sweeping the floor, yet the house was always spotless.

Down the hallway, Evelyn taped a box shut absent-mindedly and quickly carried it near her bedroom door to be picked up later by the moving crew. She was unsure if the gloomy weather was enhancing the bittersweet feelings welling up inside her. She stared at the empty shelves as she thought back to her younger years playing with Barbie dolls and using the small bedroom table to play out bakery cafe scenarios, with her younger brother, Reed, as her customer. She moved a dust cloth over the empty shelves near her bedroom window, vacuumed the carpet, and gathered the stray items that either didn't fit in a box or would have to be used last minute. Snapping into reality, Evelyn would need to hurry to finish cleaning her room before her mother called her downstairs any minute now for the trip to their new home.

The Gunderson family wasn't moving far—just forty-five minutes away by car, but it was across state lines and a distance into the countryside where her new neighbors wouldn't live right next door, but in acre-and-a-half lots a mile or more away. That's what Evelyn's parents wanted—a home on more land with less of the hustle and bustle and more time to take in the surrounding natural beauty.

Having a brand-new room in a recently constructed country house filled Evelyn with excitement. However, she had already established herself in her current school as one of the top students; she had many close friends, and her teachers loved her friendly but studious manner. Attending a new school would be scary, but she looked forward to making new friends while maintaining her current friendships; her parents had promised the children that they could reunite with their old companions for special occasions. She was also very excited to explore and take in the natural setting of her new home, which was plentiful whichever direction she looked, and try the new kitchen appliances, an upgrade from the older ones she was used to.

Evelyn was responsible for seeing that Reed was ready to go once their mother called them downstairs and making sure that he hadn't left anything behind. She knew, too, that she had to put on a brave face for Reed and keep any stray tears from falling, so she mustered a big smile and asked her brother, "All ready? Do you need any help cleaning your room? Have you been keeping an eye on Rupert? He's your responsibility, you know."

"I know," Reed answered, "Rupert, come here, boy! Go get your toy."

Rupert, the family's French bulldog, was always ready for a game of tug-of-war. He chomped on the raggedy stuffed toy that had been his go-to lately and assumed the play position, his hindquarters high in the air and his front paws firmly gripping the toy, mouth grasping it tightly, all while growling whenever a human hand came too close to take the toy away.

"Good boy, Rupert, but we're going for a ride. Do you want to go in the car, buddy?"

Rupert had learned what that phrase meant and became excited to join in any event, just as long as he was with a family member. He was always eager to accompany them anywhere, anytime.

Evelyn, an all-too-average girl who worked hard to be well above average in her accomplishments, watched Reed and Rupert playfully tussle as she fought back more tears. While she was excited to move into the new house, this was the only home she had ever known, and the familiar picture of Rupert taunting Reed to grab his toy made Evelyn smile, just as so many other memories had.

"Evelyyyyn, Reeeeeeeed, Ruperrrrt! Come downstairs; it's time to go!" Mrs. Gunderson called. "You can leave the boxes for the moving crew, and the vacuum cleaner has to stay. We'll have to come back to take care of the final cleanup before we close on the house sale. And, Evelyn, please make sure not to water any of the large houseplants; we don't want the movers to put them in the moving van with the added water. It'll just make them heavier, and it won't hurt the plants to wait another day or two to be watered."

Evelyn's mother loved indoor and outdoor plants. In fact, Mrs. Gunderson was a master gardener with beautiful landscaping skills, and once they were settled in their new home, Evelyn and her mom had plans to work together to turn the scarcely landscaped new yard into a gardening masterpiece, changing areas of the flat backyard into gardens with vegetables and lovely perennials.

"Do we need to make any stops on the way?" Reed asked anxiously. "I can hardly wait to explore the woods behind the new house. Can you imagine all the games we can play in that big yard, Evelyn? I'll really get to practice my passes with my football, and I'll have a lot of room to throw my space glider around!" Reed's toy was an all-white lightweight plastic glider that had the markings of a spaceship on its body.

"Yes, we all know how much you like–no, make that *love*–playing with that glider, Reed. In fact, I don't remember the last time you weren't carrying it around."

There was more than enough room for Evelyn and Reed to play in their new backyard, and although Evelyn thought of taking time to fly a kite one day, she was more likely to use her spare time cooking or baking.

"There's plenty of time to play later, Reed. First, we need to get unpacked and organized, and then there's a lot to do to get our new home set up."

Evelyn thought of a long list of tasks she wanted to tackle. Like her mother in many ways, she had picked up plenty of organizational traits over the years. Reed, on the other hand, was a typical ten-year-old who was probably more precocious than most boys his age.

Fortunately, Evelyn thought, *Reed and I rarely argue, and he provides a good shoulder to lean on when I need it.* Living farther from neighbors would surely give the two more time at home together.

* * *

A few days later, Evelyn looked up from the book she was reading and said, "I think the moving process went fairly smoothly, Mom. What do you think?"

"I agree, Evelyn. I know there are any number of things that could have gone wrong, but we avoided them. That's partly because your father is such a good planner like yourself, and because you helped by keeping an eye on Reed and labeling the moving boxes so well. That kept misplaced items to a minimum. Right now, I've got to get to the school for summer work, and your dad and I should be home by late afternoon. Make sure Reed doesn't sleep in too late," Mrs. Gunderson said as she grabbed her lunch and tote bag.

In their new home, Evelyn and Reed quickly established new routines. They sat eating lunch at the kitchen counter, looking outside the window at the glorious summer day, when they moved from listing items yet to be found in the unpacked boxes to talking about the beautiful views outside their new dining area. Rolling hills of countryside seemed so peaceful to Evelyn, and to Reed, they appeared to go on for miles with new shades of green trees, warmly colored fields of varied crops, and a dark green grove of pine trees that dotted the nearby acreage. The ponderosa pine trees looked as if they had been planted many years ago by someone very much like herself, Evelyn thought. Someone who was tidy and organized, because the pine trees had been planted in neat straight rows that seemed well thought out ahead of time. Mrs. Gunderson once said the pine trees reminded her of a grove very much like one near her childhood home. Although Reed had been champing at the bit to explore those pines to the point of becoming a true annoyance to the family, Evelyn was much less inclined to explore the woods.

Their parents had made good progress unpacking up to that point, so Mrs. Gunderson finally relented to Reed's persistent requests and promised that the family would take a break from house setup and have a picnic lunch in the woods that weekend, providing the weather cooperated.

Telling himself he would investigate the woods before then, Reed went to find a spot suitable for the promised picnic. He put Rupert on a lead and walked to the pine forest northeast of their house—probably a five-minute walk away. Reed stooped to pick up a large walking stick lying on the ground near the group of trees and brush that defined the back edge of their property.

"Just in case, Rupert, we'd better take along this large stick. I'm not entirely sure what wild animals are found in this area." Since their move, the family had encountered several deer crossing the road along with many wild turkeys, an opossum in the evening, and even a shy fox, so Reed fully expected that he may run into an animal if he and Rupert were quiet enough. Reed was, however, fairly certain that any larger wild creatures would be tucked far away in the woods sleeping during the day. Noise was seldom heard in the new neighborhood, with the exception of a faraway car's quiet rumble or a hammer or nail gun being used to build a new house in the distance—that is, if it wasn't too windy, which would carry the sound away.

Rupert walked ahead of Reed, sniffing the ground as the two meandered through the thicker field of high grasses. Stopping on occasion to take in the fresh air blowing the distinct smell of pine in their direction, Reed paused and took a close look at plants he had not seen before, making notes in his science notebook entitled *Reed's Collections and Observations.*

The soft wind blew gently against the hair on his neck, and when it quieted down, he tilted his head to listen to a strange sound. When the wind picked up, he and Rupert

trudged ahead, pausing to listen for the noise again. For a third time, the wind lessened, and Reed thought he heard the same odd noise. Rupert growled and barked the closer they got to the nearby pine tree forest. The strange sound was not from an animal, at least Reed was sure of that much. There was a musical quality to it, though the sound was incredibly faint, causing him to stop in his tracks to strain and listen intently for it. But the wind picked up, muffling the sound.

"Maybe we'll hear the noise better once we get closer to the forest, Rupert. The wind won't blow too much with trees around us."

The two continued their journey to the pine woods when Reed heard the noise more clearly.

"What do you think that sound could be, Rupert?" He felt his heart beating more rapidly the nearer they got to the woods. "There it is again! Did you hear that?"

Near the entrance to the woods, the wind stopped blowing altogether. Looking around to see if there was anyone or anything nearby, Reed and Rupert entered a clearing. The faint musical sounds abruptly stopped the moment Reed stepped on a larger stick, snapping it in two. At the same moment, a sudden gust of wind picked up wildly within the pines, woods smattering dust into Reed's face. As he rubbed his eyes to clean them, he looked down at Rupert to see him barking at something ahead of the two. From what Reed could see, there was nothing there but the dark shadows of larger pine trees, a blanket of fallen pine needles over the forest floor, and a bigger, thicker stick leaning against one of the trees.

As Reed's eyes focused, he noticed a small log resting against a larger pine, and he stepped as cautiously and quietly as possible, straining to hear if the quiet music had started up again. He searched up each tree near him, scoping out the entire area in front of him, when the resting log rolled over onto the forest floor, thudding loudly as it hit the ground. There was smaller, knee-high brush to contend with, and Rupert's barking sounded louder and more urgent. Reed felt another strong gust of wind pick up, followed by a flash of intense heat, making the hairs on the back of his neck stand on end.

"Why am I so scared?" he muttered, searching the trees. "We'd better head back, Rupert. I don't have a very good feeling about this."

The pair headed home with a quicker pace. All the way, Reed brushed off the dust from his hair and shirt, wondering why he had been so scared. Reed had walked through their property before without any feelings of fear or of being threatened. Was it the wind gusts, the musical sound they'd heard, or Rupert barking at something Reed couldn't see that gave him the feeling of being watched? He reached the back patio door and found his mother in the kitchen helping to prepare dinner.

"Did you check out a picnic spot, Reed?" she inquired. Looking up from her cutting board, Mrs. Gunderson got a clear look at her son and then turned to Evelyn with a curious look.

"What's all over your hair?" Evelyn asked.

"And what an odd color!" their mom added. "It even sparkles in the light." She brushed some of the glittery substance into her hands for a closer inspection.

"Whatever that stuff is, you can see how it glows, too!" added Evelyn.

Mrs. Gunderson nodded as she picked through strands of Reed's hair. She looked down at Rupert. "Why, even Rupert's fur has whatever you've got on your face and hair. You'd better get cleaned up before you bring that all over the house. You don't want your father finding that stuff on the new carpet."

Before Reed could even get a word out, his mother quickly ushered him into the bathroom, where he could see himself in the mirror. He looked paler than normal, but as he looked at his face, he saw a substance between bright glitter and sawdust all over it. He had been too scared to notice it on Rupert's fur. Bewildered, he started to wash up, scrubbing for what seemed like forever without success; the glitter dust just wasn't coming off quickly, and it was a bit sticky.

He eventually managed to remove all of it but it had taken him over an hour, and he had yet to give Rupert a bath.

"Mom, do you have anything else that I can use to clean Rupert? This stuff doesn't wash off that easily with just soap."

"Why don't you try some olive oil?" Evelyn suggested. She knew her way around the kitchen very well because of her passion for baking. "It's worth a try," she said.

"Oh, okay," Reed said, exasperated. All he wanted to do was eat dinner and get into bed, where he felt safe. Poor Rupert. The pup had been a faithful companion and guardian, and then today, he ended up a total mess, unable to clean himself up. Like any other dog, Rupert just wanted to roll on the carpet to try to remove the glittery dust in his fur. Reed hefted his stout companion into the bathtub and worked the olive oil through his fur, which worked like a charm in removing all the sticky substance. On his way back to his room, he stopped at Evelyn's door.

"Evvie, thanks for telling me about the olive oil. Did I get all that stuff out of my hair?" he asked, bending down for her to closely look at his head.

"Did you remember the bug spray? I suppose I'd better check for ticks, too. You know you've got more of that sparkly stuff in your ears to clean out, but I think I can get that right now. You look good otherwise. Where did you and Rupert pick that stuff up, anyways?"

"Oh, boy, listen to this! Rupert and I went on the strangest walk. It was real nice out, so we headed out to the pine forest. I didn't think the wind was very strong, but the closer we got to the forest, the stronger the wind kept blowing, and every now and then, the wind would stop just long enough for me to hear this really weird sound. I've never heard it before, and I'm not sure I can even describe it, but it was a musical sound, or maybe it was some mating call from one of the bugs we see around outside." Reed tried to contain his excitement so he didn't get too out of breath. "It kind of reminded me of a whale's song, but the wind kept interrupting. I can't explain it except that it was strangely musical and a little soothing at the same time. Rupert kept barking at something in the air, and then his bark got louder and stronger when we got closer to the woods." He took a breath before continuing, "As we started to enter the woods, a super strong gust of wind blew all around us, and I got the distinct feeling it was sort of a message for us to stay away. Then *poof.* All this weird glitter stuff got all over us. All I could think of was that we were going to get in trouble with Mom and Dad, but I figured they'd understand if I told them what happened—but then again, maybe not. It was such a bizarre experience, I don't know if I'd believe it if anyone else told me."

"It's bizarre, that's for sure. Maybe after you get something to eat and a good night's sleep, you'll think of what might have made that noise and sprayed that glitter."

Reed returned to the mirror to check and recheck his head from all angles to make sure Evelyn hadn't missed anything. No more glitter behind the ears. With a second mirror, he carefully checked the back of his head and his scalp, and he scanned Rupert again, too. Satisfied, he plopped on his bed and threw his space glider aimlessly while reflecting on his day in the pine forest. After a couple of minutes, he thought to jot down his experience in his science journal and retain the recent mystery evidence for future inspection and scrutiny. Reed returned to the laundry room to grab some remaining glitter substance so he could save it on a piece of tape, which he fastened to a page in his notebook. He told himself he would bring the substance to school later to be looked at with the help of a science teacher.

In spite of his fear, he found himself wanting to explore more of the forest again, without going too deep into the woods. Reed went to bed that night listing possible items to bring along the next day to avoid a repeat of the day's disaster.

Meanwhile, in the laundry room, Mrs. Gunderson was filling a large watering can with tepid water for her many plants' weekly watering. Evelyn figured her love of nature started by helping her mother care for their many house-plants. Her favorite was the Norfolk pine tree that she'd helped grow from a smaller plant at her grandfather's funeral years ago.

Evelyn lovingly dusted off the larger leaves of the banana palms and fiddle-leaf figs, being careful to not over-water the plants. Her mother shared information about each plant's preference with water and lighting; she knew the benefits that plants offered, and she even took the time to turn each plant around as it grew toward the light source.

Evelyn had so much experience with plants and gardening, she felt she might be a florist when she got older, but her real passion was baking. She loved finding new recipes and new combinations of flavors, especially when the recipe involved a new technique that she could learn and practice. Every year when her teacher asked about the number of books she'd read over the summer, Evelyn felt the need to explain why it didn't meet the teacher's expectations, as she'd spent all her spare time reading recipes and practicing new baking skills.

It helped her parents during the school year when Evelyn, who was typically in charge of the weekday dinners, planned ahead to create a meal that would last all week simply by tweaking a few ingredients. Dinner was an important part of the day when the family connected. Evelyn was a very intelligent young lady who had no problem making friends or taking on leadership roles in her classes. She carried that over to her home life, where she was in charge of her brother.

Evelyn told herself that she should step up and help watch Reed more closely the next day, to save him from another forest mishap. She made a note in her daily calendar to find time to join him not only so he'd have some supervision, but so she could determine what exactly that mysterious substance might be.

A Wave in the Pines

When Reed woke the next morning, it appeared he'd had an active night of dreaming, as his covers were strewn all over the bed and floor. Evelyn peeked inside his room through the slightly open door. Seeing Reed awake, she informed him that their parents had left for work and he'd better get Rupert fed and outside shortly. Reed lifted his head from the pillow, where more of the glittery substance was scattered all over. *Wow! I thought I had all that stuff out of my hair! Dad even gave me a thumbs-up after he inspected it.* He got dressed, made his bed, went downstairs, and, after feeding Rupert, went into the kitchen, where he found Evelyn making her special pancakes.

"You know, Evelyn, when I first woke up, I thought I had a terrible dream until I found still more of that glitter on my pillow! I'm not sure if I'll ever get all that stuff off!" Viewing his plate on the counter, Reed's attention was quickly diverted. "All right! Pancakes! My favorite!" He was glad to have a sister who loved practicing her culinary skills, and he loved being her chief taste tester even more.

As he finished his meal, he commented, "Thanks for breakfast, Evelyn. That was delicious. I could taste something different this time, but I couldn't put my finger on it. What'd you add that was new?"

Reed's tastes were expanding, and Evelyn appreciated not having a finicky brother. In fact, Reed was always open to eating new foods, as they often made a game out of trying the recipes that Evelyn experimented with.

"I'm glad you liked it," she said. "I tried adding some lemon zest; it's supposed to brighten the flavor of a recipe."

"Zest? What's that? Oh, it doesn't matter. The pancakes are super delicious." Reed wiped off the remaining crumbs from his face.

"You slept late, Reed. I already made breakfast, mixed up some cookies for our picnic tomorrow, and have a summer salad for our lunch ready in the fridge." Evelyn was quite the accomplished cook for her age. In fact, she had taken to cooking and baking when she was a toddler, helping her mom in the kitchen. "You know, I really should go with you to the pine grove and help you find a spot for the picnic. If we know what the area is like, then we can better help Mom and Dad pack for the picnic, but first, you need to get the chores done on that list Mom and Dad left for you on the counter. I'm not your babysitter, you know. Remember that you either get Mom and Dad's satisfaction or disappointment depending on how you do your job; I have quite enough that I want to get done on my own," Evelyn directed.

"What about you? Did you get a list of chores, too?"

"I don't need one. I'm old enough to remember everything Mom and Dad ask me to do."

"Yeah, I suppose you're right," admitted Reed, though he was careful not to say it too often. He wasn't always comfortable admitting his older sister was better than he was in any way. He did realize that increased knowledge came with age. There were some days, however, that he wasn't in the mood to accept that fact. "I'd rather have Mom or Dad make me a list, anyways. That way, it's less work for me." He bent down to pet Rupert before continuing, "I'm glad that you want to go with me to the forest; I'm not so sure I want to go back there by myself. It'd be nice to have Rupert with me, but having another person there might help me explain to Mom and Dad what I got in my hair!"

"You definitely don't want that to happen again! Mom and Dad are not going to stand for a repeat of that mess!" Evelyn paused thoughtfully. "Don't you think I'd get that stuff in my hair, too, if I went with you to the woods?"

Reed got up to put away his breakfast dishes. "No, I don't think so. We'll just have to enter slowly and watch for anything we brush up against. Besides, it just might've been something that the wind picked up and blew. In fact, now that I think of it"—Reed paused and looked at Evelyn, who was cleaning the dishes she'd used to make the salad—"there *was* a gust of wind that hit me, almost knocking me over. I remember it now because I thought it was very bizarre to feel a big gust of wind in the middle of the woods just before I got 'glittered.' Then it got very, very hot, kind of like when we stood next to the bonfire at Grandma and Grandpa's house by the lake."

Evelyn was intent on listening to the sensational details Reed was offering but she'd become impatient in attending to her kitchen tasks. "Oh, wow! I guess I'd have to have been there to fully appreciate the spectacle." She shook off the story and returned to her kitchen work, with Rupert waiting patiently for some morsel to fall to the floor.

"Evelyn, have you seen my space glider? I know that I played with it yesterday, and I've been looking all over for it. I tried to find it under my bed, but it wasn't there." Reed knew that Evelyn wasn't the type to purposely hide toys to spite him.

"No, I haven't seen it, but then, I haven't really been looking. I'll keep my eye out for it, though."

"Bummer. I really wanted to show it to the new neighbor boy down the road."

"Which new neighbor?"

"Next door to us—only *next door* is down the road. He's in third grade, and his family just moved into their new house a couple of weeks ago. Remember? We met his entire family at the neighborhood grill last week."

"Oh yeah," said Evelyn. "He seemed like a very nice kid, but it's hard to tell much just by a five-minute chat."

"Well, I know he likes forts and space gliders like I do. I'm hoping that I can find mine so we can have a glider contest out back." Reed set out to do his list of daily chores. When he finished, he returned to his bedroom to look again for his glider.

For what seemed the umpteenth time, he peered under his bed after searching nearly every nook and cranny of his room. He wasn't sure why he was looking under there again. Maybe he was hoping that Rupert had dropped the glider off after playtime earlier, but he also knew that wasn't the case, as Rupert likely would've broken—or at least damaged—it since he viewed all toys as fair game to play with roughly. Kneeling down with the side of his face flat on the floor to get a better vantage point, Reed lifted the edge of the bedcovers up. He spotted a spider crawling under his bed and wasted no time in handling it. Instead of smashing it, he walked to the front door to set it free outside; maybe his sister's love for nature was having an effect on him more than he cared to admit.

Back in the kitchen, Reed finished his juice.

Evelyn told him, "I'm sorry that I can't help you find your glider; I don't even recall when I last saw you with it, but it looks like we're all losing things these days. Mom said she didn't know which was more frustrating—not being able to find an item that was packed or not remembering where she put it in our new house."

"I know. That's why you were always reminding me to carefully label every box I packed," Reed said with a small amount of irreverence. "Hey, did you ever find the necklace Grandma gave you? I saw you wearing it a couple of days ago."

"No. I tried to go back over my steps that day, and I looked everywhere in my room. I still can't find my favorite spatula either," Evelyn said as she read the list of lost items her mom had written. Looking it over, she announced, "Mom's also looking for her favorite book and the teapot a neighbor gave her, and Dad lost the keys to his briefcase."

"Do you suppose we should name our new home the 'Loser House'?" Reed chuckled at his own joke. "I know what you're gonna say. 'This is a super nice house.' Mom and Dad are always talking about how much we all like this new house. I like it, too, but I just wish we wouldn't lose so many things in it. Summer vacation will be over before we know it, and the new school year will start, and I won't have much time to search for my space glider then."

Evelyn thought for a moment. "I think we should make our own lists of what we can't find. There are still a couple of boxes in the garage left to unpack, you know, and we can check each item off the list once we find them." Changing the subject, she asked, "Do you want to go check out a spot for tomorrow's picnic with me in a little while? Or we could just find a flat spot in the field. I know you scouted areas with Rupert, but you didn't say you found a spot. I suppose you got distracted with the glittering episode."

"Sure, but I want to go back to the pine woods with you because I need fort material. I was planning on picking up any good-size pieces of wood for my collection," Reed answered. "Dad said that we could all help bring some wood back to the yard, and he'd help cut the pieces for me to use later."

"That'll take a lot of time and a lot of wood, and with Dad working full-time, he won't be able to do much to help with your fort. He's already had to fix some of the smaller issues around here, like the problem with the ice. There's still a lot of setup work to be done."

"Back up, Evvie. Who has a problem with ice? What ice?"

"It's the strangest thing. There's been a pile of ice cubes in Rupert's dish every day. Dad wondered if you or I put them there. He even asked Mom if she was feeding Rupert ice cubes!" The image made Evelyn smile before she turned to Reed with seriousness. "You aren't, are you?"

"Of course not! That'd mean I'd have to clean melting ice out of his dish, and I'm never in the mood to make extra work for myself."

"Then that's a mystery we should help Dad solve, but how strange is it that ice cubes are showing up in Rupert's dish?"

Putting that thought aside, Evelyn needed to bake a cake. She was already in the middle of measuring ingredients. Her mom had helped her prepare a menu for that night and the next day's picnic before she'd left for work that morning. Evelyn's enthusiasm for learning the latest and greatest culinary techniques seemed to grow with every dish she created, and she wanted to be at the top of her game to make an entry for the county fair, which was just around the corner.

As she cleaned up her morning dishes, she inadvertently knocked her mom's favorite coffee mug on the floor, breaking it into many small pieces. Her heart sank. She knew how special the mug was to her, as Evelyn had given it to her for Mother's Day just a couple of months earlier. She brokenheartedly swept the shattered pieces into a pile and set them on a paper towel on the counter, promising herself that she would confess later that night. Meanwhile, she could try piecing it together, but that thought was interrupted as she heard Reed shriek from his room. She trudged upstairs to see what the problem was, and as she reached his room, she found Reed sliding his body from under his bed. "Look, Evelyn! My space glider! It was under my bed!"

"What? You said you couldn't find it there earlier," Evelyn stated with a little confusion.

"I looked under my bed many times," Reed said. "There was definitely no glider there. In fact, I know it wasn't there. I was just bending down to put on my socks, and out of the corner of my eye, I saw a glimmer of light under my bed near the back wall, and that's where I found the glider, way in the corner, all the way back where I could barely reach it." Reed was mystified as to how his lost glider hadn't been under his bed all the times he'd looked before.

"Well, I'm glad that mystery is solved. Now let me finish my work in the kitchen. The less you interrupt me, the faster I finish!"

Reed also wondered what may have caused the brief glimpse of light he'd seen when he'd looked under the bed, but he dismissed the thought as he excitedly made plans to go outside to practice throwing his newly found toy. He set his glider on the chair in his room and used both hands to secure it, making a special mental note of where he was leaving it so he'd know where to find it later. While reaching for Rupert's leash, which was resting on the desk in Reed's room, he could see in his peripheral vision that the newly found space glider was beginning to disappear again. His head whipped around to quickly catch sight of the toy before it vanished. He looked down and around the room to see if the glider had drifted onto the floor, but there was no glider in sight. Looking under his bed again, thinking maybe he had just imagined finding it there earlier, he saw only darkness. His eyes returned to the desk chair where he had set his glider, and Reed saw that it was back where he had put it moments earlier.

"Evelynnnnn!" Reed was miffed, thinking that Evelyn was somehow playing tricks on him.

Evelyn called up to Reed's room, "What do you want now, Reed?"

Reed shouted back, "Hey, how did you get down there so fast?"

"Down where? I've been here the whole time working on my cakes." *And Mom's cup,* she added to herself. Evelyn was confused as to what was going on with Reed, and although she was still busy in the kitchen, she didn't want to miss a possible emergency. She trotted up to his room and repeated the question as she entered Reed's room. "What are you talking about?"

"I thought you took my space glider after I *just* set it on my desk chair. I turned around, and then it was gone. When I looked around again for it, I couldn't find anywhere in my room, and when I looked back at the chair . . . well, there it was!"

They simultaneously looked at the space glider resting on the chair as the toy flickered in and out of view. It appeared as if there was bad reception in the air until the glider disappeared fully again. They gaped at the spot where the glider had just been, and before either could utter a word, the glider reappeared. They looked at each other in bewilderment and then back to the glider.

"Hey, are you playing with me, Reed?"

"No, honestly. I'm not doing a thing. I don't have a clue how it could be there one second and then disappear. Maybe our eyes are just tricking us, or maybe there's a problem with the lighting in the room."

"Reed, things just don't disappear and then reappear, and there's a lot of outdoor light coming in because it's sunny outside."

"I know, but how else could this happen?" Reed wasn't scared, only mystified as he went to grab his toy before it disappeared again.

"Oh, I don't know, Reed. I don't have much time to think about it now; I've got to get back to the kitchen to get my cakes out of the oven." She didn't have any more patience to deal with a space glider, and she heard the oven timer go off in the distance.

Returning to the kitchen, she turned on the oven light to see if she could view the cakes without opening the oven door, because she knew that would make the temperature drop, preventing her cakes from having a beautiful golden finish. Opening the oven door might also cause her cakes to collapse if done too prematurely, and she could see that they needed just a few more minutes to bake. She put the recipes for the picnic away and tidied up the kitchen. By now, she had forgotten about the reappearing glider, and she turned her attention back to the broken cup. After retrieving glue from the craft room cupboard, Evelyn went to the kitchen counter, where she had set all the pieces of Mrs. Gunderson's broken cup.

Evelyn gasped and stood astonished as she stared at the counter for several minutes.

The cup no longer appeared broken, nor even cracked.

"Reeeed!" Putting her hands to her hips, she wondered if Reed was paying her back for the disappearing and reappearing glider.

Reed jogged into the kitchen and replied, "What do you want?"

"Mom's favorite cup fell earlier and broke. Did you put it back together again?"

"No, but I'm telling Mom you broke it," Reed teased. Evelyn knew that he wasn't serious. Reed added, "Seriously, I didn't even know that there was a broken cup until you just told me."

"I'll have to check with Mom and Dad to see what these keys are for, too. I came across them when I returned books to the shelf," Evelyn muttered.

"What keys? Can I see them?"

"They're over there by the charging station for the phone. You know, where Mom and Dad usually sit when they pay bills."

Reed walked over to the keys and analyzed them. "These look like the ones to Dad's briefcase. We'd better call him and let him know."

Just then, Rupert began barking loudly and scratching at the cupboard door to try to get at something inside. Reed opened the cupboard to find baking pans stacked orderly. He adjusted a couple of pans to get a look at what might have caused Rupert to bark, but nothing seemed out of place.

"I don't know what you want, Rupert. There's nothing there except baking pans."

Reed shut the cupboard, but before he had a chance to get out of the kitchen, Rupert was barking at the cupboard again. Reed rolled his eyes and searched the cupboards once more to show Rupert that there was nothing to bark about. Rupert stopped, sniffed the cupboard area, and stepped back while Reed looked at Evelyn for an explanation.

"It's kind of an odd morning, Reed, don't you think?" Evelyn sat at the kitchen table to make a checklist for their picnic. "Your mysterious glider, Mom's cup, Rupert seeing something that we can't see." She paused. "And the small set of keys by the cookbooks that I know wasn't there earlier, because I had *just* returned two cookbooks to the shelf a few minutes ago."

Reed mumbled before swallowing some toast, "You'll have to ask Dad about the keys. Be careful, Evelyn. You'll have to be on your toes. You wouldn't want something to disappear and then suddenly show up."

"Like your glider," she quipped. "And if these are the keys belonging to Dad's briefcase, then he'll be able to get the papers in there for work."

Reed absent-mindedly reflected on the morning's events.

"All done," Evelyn announced. "The cakes are on a baking rack cooling off. I made our family's favorite cake for us and for Mom's new friend at the end of the road. Before I can frost them, the cakes will have to cool down quite a bit, so if you want to go to the grove of pine trees now, I can join you." Evelyn placed her cookbook down, using a bookmark to save the recipe she was viewing. "Shall we take Rupert along?"

"No," Reed said without hesitation. "If we get hit again with that glitter stuff, I don't want to have to spend time cleaning him up, too! I'm sure he'll need a midday nap, anyways."

"I'll get my tennis shoes while you call Dad about the keys."

Reed called his dad and left a message about the keys. Then he headed upstairs. Absent-mindedly, he went through the motions of brushing his teeth while thinking back to the discovery of the glider beneath his bed. He remembered seeing that glimmer of light just before he spotted the glider in the dark corner under the bed, and then he recalled hearing a distinct bell chime. He pondered what might have made the sound as he returned to his room to investigate, but he became entirely distracted when he found the bed he had made neatly before coming down to breakfast was all disheveled now. *Hey! I know I made my bed this morning.* His initial thought was that Rupert had been on his bed, but it was too high for Rupert to jump on. *How did my bed get messed up like that when I was downstairs? Evelyn was either in the kitchen or with me this morning. Rupert must have somehow jumped high enough.*

Marching back down to the kitchen, Reed blurted out to Evelyn, "Where's Rupert? He messed up my bed after I already made it this morning, before I came down to breakfast." Reed, clearly upset, forgot all about looking into what might have caused the bell chime sound.

"Rupert's been at my feet while I've been in the kitchen. You know how he is about keeping the floor clean whenever I cook or you eat. He's always hoping for a handout. What's got you all riled up?" Evelyn inquired.

"I thought Rupert went back upstairs while I was eating breakfast. Did you go back upstairs and mess up my bed?" The morning was proving to be a little taxing on their nerves, and they weren't sure what make of it all.

"I've been down here in the kitchen all morning trying to work on my cakes. You know that! I was either with you or down here the whole time; besides, how could you forget that your bed's too high up for Rupert to jump on?" Now it was Evelyn who was a little miffed after so many interruptions. "You know that I don't do those kinds of pranks." Evelyn took pride in acting mature for her age, and she considered it a great compliment whenever people who were newly introduced to her mentioned it.

Reed returned to his room, grumbling to himself as made his bed for the second time that day. He was absolutely positive that he had made it earlier, and there wasn't a possibility that Rupert or Evelyn messed it up. "I think my mind is playing tricks on me," he muttered to himself.

It was time to redirect their attention from the questionable happenings at home to the pine woods. Evelyn and Reed gathered Reed's walking stick and headed toward the woods. The sunny day warmed up the temperature quickly, and because it was a particularly humid day, Evelyn thought to bring a water bottle. Taking in the beauty of the field and soaking up the sounds of the various birds chirping, tweeting, and singing out their calls, she followed Reed. The picnic spot had to be fairly level and fairly well lit.

Reed said, "I know where there's a very good spot for the picnic, and I think the ground is mostly flat in the place I have in mind. You'd get some shade, which would be a little cooler if the weather is hot like today. It's only a little ways into the woods."

As they slowly entered the pine woods, a big gust of wind blew from behind them, chilling them instantly. They looked at each other, wondering where the wind came from, because the air had been quiet, hot, and stifling until that point.

"Did you feel that?" Evelyn asked Reed as she looked around. "That was one of the coldest breezes that I've ever felt on a hot day!"

"I told you that these woods are a little spooky," Reed said suspiciously as he surveyed their surroundings. "I also get a feeling that someone's watching even though I can't see anybody else here."

"Mom and Dad will appreciate the quietness of the pine woods, but I agree. I think it's a little scary."

She picked up a plastic bag that had made its way into the woods, knowing that she was not only doing good but also setting an example for Reed. She figured it would be nice for forest life if she did her part to help Mother Nature. Reed, on the other hand, wasn't as attentive. Instead, he was focused solely on showing Evelyn the area he had in mind for the picnic. They went their own separate directions for a short time, stepping over small brush and weeds.

When they both felt they'd spent enough time in the woods to get acquainted sufficiently with the area, Reed announced, "There, Evelyn. That's the spot I think would be super for the picnic." He pointed to a level clearing with scarce pine needles, brush, and weeds.

Evelyn surveyed the spot and agreed. "Since there are very few overhanging branches, it'll be open but still provide us a little shade. I'm excited to show Mom and Dad our picnic spot, and I know they'll find it peaceful and relaxing. There won't be other people blocking any views like whenever we picnicked at the beach."

The two explored the area a bit more. Evelyn took in the views all around her, being quiet, as it might result in seeing something special.

"Shhh, Reed! Talk softly so we don't disturb any animals," she said.

She didn't pay attention to whether or not Reed was following her advice, because she couldn't take her eyes off the small pine branch that appeared to be waving to her. She stood frozen until she nudged Reed and whispered, "Look up over there. It looks like that small tree branch is waving at us."

Reed's eyes quickly found the lone, swaying tree branch Evelyn was referring to. "It *is* waving at us! None of the other branches are moving on that tree, and there's no breeze in these woods to move branches."

They inched quietly toward the waving branch, never taking their eyes off it. Something was behind it! At first, it looked like a small animal, but upon closer inspection, it wasn't; it was a small fluorescent being with wings, but that was all they could make out, and within moments, it disappeared.

"You *did* see that, Reed, right? I mean, I just can't be imagining this. I thought I saw a . . . well, I'm not sure what I saw, but it was small, bright, very fast moving, and it had wings."

"I saw the same thing that you saw, but I have no clue what it was! I really don't think it was a bird or an animal. Of course, there seem to be a thousand different kinds of bugs, too. Let's get home and see if we can find out what it was while it's still fresh in our memories."

The two rushed back home with Reed holding the

walking stick tightly and Evelyn carrying the stray white plastic trash bag she'd picked up, waving it against the breeze.

3.

Cake Capers

Filled with bewilderment and perhaps even a little fear at the thought of returning to the forest later, the children worked fervently on Evelyn's laptop to research the unusual creature they had encountered in the pines. Finding out what small wildlife lived in the forest seemed like a good place to start.

"Hmm. Look up bats, Reed. That might explain what we saw." Evelyn's mind raced to many other possibilities.

"No, I know what bats look like, and that thing on the branch was clearly not a bat. What about an unusual insect? Do you think that thing might have been a strange bug? They come in all different colors and sizes, you know, and this thing was super bright, remember? It almost glowed!" Reed recalled. He wanted to hurry and find something that came close to what they saw on the branch before the image began to disappear from his mind. It was easy to get distracted, as more information led to other pictures that had nothing to do with their original search. "I'm trying to stay focused, Evelyn."

"And I'm trying to think of all sorts of possibilities. The larger our scope of probable subjects, the greater the chance of landing on the one that we're looking for." Evelyn surprised herself at how scientific she sounded.

Reed looked back to Evelyn and pointed out, "You know, Ev, your way is not always the right way!"

"I didn't say that my way was the right way or even the best way. I'm just trying to think of more options to increase the likelihood of finding what we saw before I waste any more time arguing with you and the image escapes my mind, too."

They reviewed all sorts of insects on the computer. They looked up birds as well, but nothing came close to what they'd seen.

"I've got an idea! Reed, you draw what you think you saw, and I'll draw what I think I saw. We'll be as detailed as possible while it's fresh in our memories and take as long as we need to."

They began to sketch, then colored in the details.

"I'm almost done with my drawing, Reed. How about you?"

"I'm almost done, too, except I can't find a crayon that'll best match the color I saw on that thingamajig," Reed said. "Some fluorescent crayons would be perfect for my drawing."

"I think we're both recalling the unique color. Let's compare our drawings."

Their drawings were very similar, indeed. Evelyn looked at Reed's picture and back to hers, examining each again and again. Eventually, she announced, "I've got it! Look up fairies on the computer. That tree or forest thing reminds me of a picture of a fairy I once saw."

"There's no such thing as fairies, and if it were really a fairy, there wouldn't be a soul who'd believe you," Reed warned.

"Just look it up. You never know what we might come across. Besides, we've been looking on the computer for over an hour without any luck." Evelyn moved Reed aside and typed *fairy* into the computer. Lists and images turned up on their screen. "Look! I told you! Our drawings kind of look like this picture of a fairy." She pointed to a picture bearing striking similarities to what they had witnessed in the woods.

The website had pictures of other creatures that looked like fairies as well: pixies, elves, spirits, sprites, and more. Reed read aloud the definition of fairy. "'A small imaginary being of a human form that has magical powers, especially a female one.' See? It says right there in the definition that it's immmmaaagginnnnary!" He stretched the word out in emphasis.

They clicked on other links, leading them to find several different names for fairies and such beings. Neither Evelyn nor Reed could find a complete match to their drawings, but they decided to print the image of the fairy that most looked like what they'd seen.

The considerable time researching left their minds full and in need of a diversion. "We'd better get back to reality for now," Evelyn said. "I've got another cake to make for Mom's work friends and get the other cakes frosted, and Dad wants you to get what we need to go on the picnic gathered up so that we're ready to go tomorrow."

"Oh, all right. After I get those picnic items ready to go for tomorrow, I want to go out and walk down to that neighbor boy and see if he wants to play. I'll bring Rupert."

"I don't think that's a good idea. Don't you remember what Mom said about taking Rupert out on walks when it's this hot outside? Frenchies don't do well in this heat," Evelyn said as she began assembling her ingredients for the cake.

Reed protested, "It's not that far, Evelyn. My friend lives at the end of our road. Surely, I can walk that far by myself." But he opted not to take a risk with Rupert's health; he didn't want to give Evelyn any opportunity to say, *"I told you so."*

"You'd better take a phone with you just in case. I'll be here busy making my cake." Evelyn proceeded to butter the cake pan while Reed went on his way to play with the neighbor.

She proceeded to add the ingredients one after another into the mixing bowl all while thinking back to the fairy that she saw on the Internet. She tried to concentrate on the steps and ingredients, but the encounter with the strange forest creature would not leave her thoughts. "Oh no," Evelyn thought out loud. "What am I doing? This cake will never turn out the way it's supposed to! I'm having such a hard time keeping my mind focused on these baking steps. I forgot how many eggs I added."

She proceeded to count the eggshells she had tossed in the garbage, but some weren't broken neatly in half, and it was simply too difficult to match the shell parts to whole eggs. Just as she was thinking of starting the cake-making process over again, an egg popped out of the carton and rolled toward her, levitated itself just over the bowl, and split in two, spilling its soft, thick contents over the cake mixture. Evelyn gaped, not knowing what to make of the egg cracking itself into a bowl.

"No one's going to believe this!" she said.

She must have been feeling light-headed; she shook off the incident and continued working, hoping the cake would turn out rather than her wasting all the ingredients by starting over.

After the oven timer went off, Evelyn pulled out the cake and sighed with relief. "This is fabulous! This cake looks just gorgeous!" she exclaimed. After kitchen clean-up, she set the cake out to cool, prepared the frosting, covered the bowl, and set it aside.

"Reed should be on his way home by now," she mumbled to herself.

Leaving to check, she headed to the end of their driveway, where she could see him walking down the road toward her. She decided to wait there for him so that she could share the egg incident with him.

"How was your time with your new friend?" she asked.

"It was great! Gary–that's his name–he's a third grader. He seems pretty cool, and we had a lot of fun playing with my space glider! In fact, he's going to ask his parents for one of his own. Then we can have some backyard competitions and race our gliders!" Reed's enthusiasm was clear.

Evelyn could hardly contain herself. "Reed! You'll never believe what just happened in the kitchen when I was baking my cake! It was the strangest thing. I was trying to mix the cake batter, but I couldn't stop thinking about that forest creature we saw earlier. Well, I lost count of how many eggs I added, so I tried to think of how best to solve the problem, when an egg suddenly started rising up from the carton! It rolled on the counter, and then cracked itself open into the cake mix all by itself!" She could hardly believe what she was saying.

Normally, Reed would have laughed at her and suggested that she was losing her mind, but after all the strange things that had happened recently, his interest was dramatically heightened. He stopped in his tracks. "Cool! I wonder who made that happen? What did you do after that?"

"I didn't know what to do! I sort of froze and stared at the whole display. I just kept trying to think of an explanation for it, and since I couldn't think of one, I just pretended it didn't happen until I could talk to you about it," she replied breathlessly.

"Don't you think that we should tell Mom and Dad?" Reed asked.

"No. Besides, they would never believe us."

"But they'd probably help identify that forest thingamajig we saw yesterday, and they might be able to explain these weird happenings around here."

"If we tell Mom and Dad, they might scare away the creatures or whatever they are."

Reed thought about that. "Well"–he paused for a moment–"you just don't know what you don't know!"

"What? What's that supposed to mean?" Evelyn's patience was disappearing like the early-morning puddles drying up in the heat of the high afternoon temperatures. "You know how parents can spoil things sometimes. I just don't want to risk scaring away something that might come around if we give it time, and there's a real possibility that if Mom and Dad know what that creature is, they won't allow us to go back to the forest."

"I suppose." Reed felt a little defeated, and he didn't like it when he and Evelyn disagreed; they got along so well, balancing each other out while appreciating the other's differences. After additional thought, he added, "Whatever those forest creatures are . . . well, they'd probably be less afraid of you and me. Mom and Dad are bigger than we are, and they'd probably not be as open as we are to new creatures."

"I think you see my point, Reed."

They walked into the house, set Reed's glider down, and headed for the kitchen to cool off with refreshing beverages. Reed poured himself a glass of water, spilling it when Evelyn screamed loudly. "Now why would you scare me like that? You made me spill water all over the counter!" Reed exclaimed.

"Reed, look at my cake!"

"Yeah, so?"

Evelyn continued to explain, stuttering, "When I . . . when I left the cake . . . well, it was just a cake on the rack waiting to cool off so that I could frost it. Now look at it. It's assembled and frosted!" She turned to face Reed. "I didn't frost this cake; I only made the frosting, which I left in a bowl. I planned on frosting it after I walked you home from your friend's house."

"Well, maybe you forgot. It is pretty hot outside, you know. Maybe the heat got to your head and you're a little delirious," Reed suggested. Then, as an afterthought, he stopped again, turning to Evelyn. "I'm getting a little spooked. There's getting to be quite a number of weird things happening with this new house."

"I know, but I don't think it's just this house. I think it's the forest, too."

They stood staring at the beautifully frosted cake. They looked around the kitchen to find whatever had frosted and assembled the cake. Without knowing what else to do, Reed continued to clean up the spilled water, and Evelyn covered all of her cakes to keep them fresh.

Reed answered the phone as he watched Evelyn put the cakes away. "Hello? Oh, hi, Dad. Yep, I finished with those jobs on the list. Thanks, but we're doing just fine. Nope. Rupert's fine, too. Okay, can I wait to work on helping you organize the garage tonight? Great. Bye . . . No, wait, one more thing, Dad. Did you ever find your briefcase keys? No? I think we came across them this morning. Sure, I'll talk to you later, Dad." Reed set the phone down and relayed their father's directions. "Dad said that he wants you to set the keys you found in a safe place and that you're supposed to make my bed for me for the rest of the week."

"He did not!"

Reed laughed out loud. "No, but I was serious about the keys, and I still think that telling Mom and Dad about these tiny creatures is a good idea." Reed left the room.

Evelyn furrowed her eyebrows more deeply and bit the inside of her cheek as she did whenever she faced difficult choices. Perhaps by not responding to Reed's idea of sharing their mysterious encounter and happenings, it would all disappear.

With the cakes completed, they were ready for the picnic. One of the cakes was intended for their mom's friend, Mrs. Jenson, which she picked up before afternoon's end.

Later in the evening, Mrs. Jenson called Evelyn.

"Evelyn, thank you for helping me by making that cake. My family thought it the *most* delectable cake ever. It was moist and beautiful, and it had such a wonderfully unique flavor! I'd love the recipe, but I suppose the cake wouldn't taste as good if I made it," Mrs. Jenson said.

Evelyn was used to getting compliments for her baking, but she was a little uncertain how this cake would have tasted. She had managed to complete the cake after messing up the ingredients, and who knew how it tasted after it had been inexplicably frosted and assembled? Had it even been safe to eat?

"Thank you, Mrs. Jenson. I appreciate your kind words. Enjoy the rest of the cake, and let me know if I can help out with anything else." Evelyn hoped and prayed that the cakes were, indeed, safe to eat and that she had frosted them while so deep in thought that she hadn't recalled completing them. What was she thinking? She knew she had never frosted a cake as beautifully as the cakes she'd seen earlier in the kitchen. She had always aspired to frost as professional bakers do, but her hands were not as controlled as she hoped, and these cakes showed an expertise that she knew she didn't have. She only wished she could decorate cakes so well.

"Oh, Evelyn, I think you are being far too modest,"

Mrs. Jenson assured Evelyn. "I'll make sure your skills are well advertised, so be prepared for more business."

* * *

Saturday morning arrived, and the family set out at lunchtime to picnic as planned. Every family member helped in carrying the picnic supplies as they set off toward the picnic site. Mr. Gunderson commented, "I sure appreciate that you and Reed were able to get this picnic organized by yourselves; it helps a lot that we can not only trust you two when we're working, but also rely on you to follow directions."

Mrs. Gunderson inquired, "Did you make a checklist so you didn't forget to pack anything?"

"Of course I did, Mom. That's the only way I can remember everything." Evelyn looked at Reed as she said this to see if he was picking up on the advice. He just rolled his eyes, knowing how often Evelyn spoke with a message intended for his ears. Mr. Gunderson rubbed Reed's head as he smiled broadly. Their eyes met with the unspoken understanding of Mrs. Gunderson and Evelyn's message.

The family walked on what had now become an easily recognizable path to the pine forest. It was decided that Rupert would stay home, where it was much cooler, and Reed had been instructed to be utterly careful carrying the cake.

"This'll be so fun," Evelyn said, smiling broadly. She had been looking forward to this opportunity since they moved in; however, she felt some apprehension wondering what surprises they might find in the forest. Would they see that waving creature again? Would they find more glitter?

"I can't wait to show you the perfect spot we found for our picnic," Reed said, leading the family the short distance to the picnic area near the forest entrance. He waved away a couple of fast-moving large bugs, which flew around his ears, just missing his head. He could hear the rapid beating of their wings and feel his hair move as he continued to brush them away. Looking toward the insects, he could see one of these bugs hovering for a brief instant in midair. It hovered just long enough for Reed to clearly see the creature had a tiny human face attached to a tiny body with fluttering wings. He heard it whisper "Go back" before quickly flying off again.

It took some time to register, as Reed could not believe this small flying being actually existed. Perhaps it was an insect, or was it a hummingbird species he had never seen before? He looked ahead to where Evelyn was walking and quickened his stride to motion to her that he had seen something of importance. His eyes told Evelyn that something was amiss, and he whispered, "I have something to tell you later."

After the five-minute walk, the family arrived at the edge of the forest. They stopped talking and looked down at the ground. At first, what they saw looked like a scattering of sticks, but as they continued looking steadily, the sticks seemed to form letters. The family looked at each other quizzically. Dad pointed to each letter, sounding out the message,

"S-T-A-Y O-U-T. Did one of you two write this message?" Mr. Gunderson inquired with clear dismay in his voice.

Mrs. Gunderson was not at all amused either.

"No, we had nothing to do with that message," Evelyn assured her parents.

"Not only would I not know where to find all those small sticks, I wouldn't have the patience either," Reed added.

"Hmm, I wonder who else is walking around this area," Mrs. Gunderson thought aloud.

The family continued on to the picnic spot. Mrs. Gunderson laid out the blanket and set the food out while they all looked over their shoulders. The message had caused a troubling tone for the picnic, but they continued to make the most of their time together.

Mr. Gunderson commented, "Thanks for your help, Reed, in finding this perfect spot! And you did a super job making us lunch, Evelyn. That salad hit the spot, and this cake is out of this world!" He swallowed his mouthful before asking, "Is this something Mom helped you with?"

Before Evelyn could respond, her mom added, "Yes, Evelyn! This is one of the most extraordinary cakes I've ever tasted! I can't put my finger on why it's so delicious. Maybe it's your secret ingredient–love–that you put into it. I think I want a second piece. It's scrumptious!"

Evelyn beamed with pride. "I'm glad you like it so much. I almost didn't think it was going to work out, because I lost my concentration on how much of each ingredient I added and thought maybe I messed up. I also worried this heat might ruin the frosting, but for some reason, it hasn't seemed to affect the cake." It was relief that Evelyn felt primarily, but she, too, thought there was something different about the cake, as it was elevated somehow to a more sophisticated flavor than she remembered this recipe ever having before. Could the mysterious egg handler have added something to this cake along with the extra egg?

"Thank you, kids, for a relaxing afternoon," Mr. Gunderson said approvingly. "This is a fine picnic spot you found, and with the delicious lunch, well, it made for a lovely afternoon."

The earlier warning to get out had been put on the wayside as Mrs. Gunderson reclined with her head on her husband's chest, his head lying on his arm on the picnic blanket. They rested after tidying up the picnic mess, and Reed looked around and studied each tree carefully to see if there was any evidence of the fairylike creature they had glimpsed earlier. The peacefulness of the afternoon seemed to go on for hours—if only it weren't for another one of those large "bugs" zooming around Reed's head. Reed brushed it away repeatedly, but soon, another very large insect descended in front of Reed's view. This time, it slowed just long enough for Reed to see that it was not a large insect of any sort but rather a thin, dragonfly-sized creature flying with a fluorescent underbelly. Reed quickly poked Evelyn and directed her attention toward this stunning creature. The kids just stared at the flitting being, trying to make out just what it might be, but it was apparent to Evelyn.

"Reed," Evelyn whispered, "that looks very similar to one of those fairies we saw on the Internet."

The quietness of the forest allowed the children to hear the scolding words of the flying fairy. "Get out! This is *our* sacred area!" And with that, the fairy darted off and disappeared.

Mr. Gunderson glanced at the children, who looked as if they had seen a ghost, and asked, "Evelyn, did you say something?"

Evelyn looked at Reed. "Uh, I was just telling Reed to finish collecting our picnic trash."

"Yes, we had all better pitch in," Mrs. Gunderson added. "We've been here all afternoon, and we'd better get back to Rupert." The picnic area was cleaned up with nary a crumb left behind, although the ground that the family picnicked on was jostled about. With the parents' approval that the site had been cleaned up adequately, the family left for their short walk home.

The energy in the pine forest changed soon after the Gunderson family left; a thunderous cloud wafted among the pine trees, and then flashes of lightning sparkled, darting in and out of the clouds as if tiny luminescent toothpicks were falling between the clouds and down to the pine forest floor. The winds picked up quickly and died down just as rapidly, as if the forest breathed with disapproval.

4.

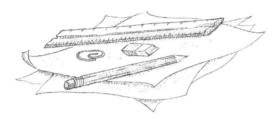

Prisoner Plans

"Hey, Evelyn! I've got the greatest idea!" announced Reed, entering Evelyn's room while brushing his teeth.

Naturally, Evelyn, with her left eyebrow raised in mild disapproval, had difficulty making out every word between the swishing of his toothbrush. "Hold that thought, Reed. Finish brushing your teeth, and then come back to tell me what your idea is." Once again, Evelyn found herself sounding like her parents.

Excited, Reed returned quickly. "I figured out what we can do to find out, once and for all, what that fluorescent fairy thing is in the woods. I'll make a trap, and we can catch it!" He thought his idea was a fairly good one, but children his age don't often think things through, as Evelyn reminded him.

"Just how do you plan to do that? Don't you remember how fast that thing was? We could barely make out what it was, and I know because it paused in front of me, too, while it was warning us. Also, don't forget that when you trap something, there's usually bait involved. You'll want to entice it. What do you plan on using to trap this thing?"

"Well, give me some time. I just thought of the trapping idea. Don't worry; I'll think of something that might attract this fairy thing," announced Reed. "First, I'll find something that I can use as the trap, or I'll build it from scratch, and then I'll put something inside that should bring in that creature—let's just call it a *fairy* for now."

"Good luck with that." Evelyn was sure Reed wouldn't have any luck with his idea. "I mean, really, Reed. Your first hurdle is to figure out what in the world would attract a fairy to a small cage. Then the cage has to be designed to close exceptionally fast so that the little speed demon doesn't get away."

"Just wait. You'll be surprised what a lot of determination can do. I can be pretty mighty even though I'm the smallest one in our family." Turning to go to his room, Reed said a prayer to himself that he would be successful, even if just to prove to his sister that he could accomplish whatever he set his mind to.

He went to bed concentrating so hard on trapping that he could hardly fall asleep, but the intense focus did result in his morning announcement to Evelyn, popping his head into her room: "I may not have my fairy trap built yet, but I know what would attract it to the trap!"

"Huh? Oh, good morning, Reed." Evelyn paused, to let the neurons in her brain make more connections before continuing. "You know, you just woke me up." She was still very groggy though her alarm clock was about to go off. "So what is it that attracts fairies?" Evelyn turned her head into the pillow. "Go ahead, I'm still listening."

Reed entered her room and sat down on a chair by her desk, the morning sunlight streaming in beneath the drawn shades. "I could hardly sleep last night 'cause all I could think about was the fairy trap. If you remember when we first saw the fairy in the forest, it was waving at us behind the pine tree branch. I thought I'd start by putting a few pine needles in the cage, because it might make the trap seem more like a home to the captive. Then I thought I'd add some glitter." Reed smiled with pride at what the idea he viewed as particularly clever.

Evelyn's head popped up from the pillow. "Glitter? Why would a fairy be attracted to glitter? And you'd better be careful not to get any in the house. You remember how frustrated Mom was from your first visit to the pine woods!"

"I know! That's what made me think of glitter. I figure since they like using the stuff on me, they are probably very familiar with it. Think about the fluorescent color, too. Maybe with glitter and something shiny, it might attract one of them." Reed paused reflectively. "Evelyn, I've got nothing to lose and maybe a fairy, or whatever it is, to gain."

Evelyn pushed her face into her pillows.

Reed continued, "Now I need to work on the construction of the cage. You know I'm great at building forts. Do you want to help me?" He thought two minds were better than one, and perhaps, if he and Evelyn worked together, the contraption would be built faster. Like most fourth graders, patience was not Reed's virtue.

"Not now, Reed. I've got to get ready for church, and you should, too."

"Oh, that's right, it's Sunday."

The Gunderson family found their church to be a great place to engage with each other and their new neighbors.

"Then I'll have to put my plans on hold until after lunch."

* * *

Reed tried with all his might to concentrate on the church sermon, but his mind was preoccupied, although he did pray for a little help in the success of capturing new prey.

He ate his lunch while organizing and looking over his doodles of the trap. Arranging all the drawings and numbering them to keep them orderly, he spent the entire afternoon on combining part of one idea with parts from others. It wasn't long before he finally had a model of what he thought might turn out to be a successful trap.

Evelyn then helped him gather materials. Thrilled with the final construction of his fairy trap, he thought that he'd made it unique. He had gone with the easiest option but was proud that it was completely his idea. In

the garage, he had found a clay flowerpot that had a small crack and a chip missing; he'd attached a paper clasp inside it that would act as a hinge. At the top of the large crack, he'd added a piece of cardboard, creating a door to prevent anything trapped from escaping, and to the bottom, he put a small, flat square piece of wood to help create stability wherever it was placed. He thought there would be sufficient room to draw in a curious fairy creature, with any movement such as a slight wind causing the trapdoor to fall.

Reed and Evelyn set out to the pine forest, looking for the perfect tree with a limb to place the trap on. It had to be up relatively high, which was not a matter for Reed to worry about, as he considered himself a master tree climber. He found what he thought was a perfect branch to hold the trap, nestled the structure, and secured it to ensure it would not fall, even on a windy night.

Climbing up was always easier than getting down. With the help of Evelyn's shoulders, Reed worked his way to the pine-covered ground, groaning as he stepped onto the forest floor.

"Oh no, Evelyn. I have to go back up! I forgot to put the bait inside the cage."

Evelyn rolled her eyes and reached into her pocket for the box of glitter, which she'd helped Reed remember to bring. He took out a small, shiny bell he had found at home and swiftly climbed back up to the trap to insert both the bell and a small pile of glitter, climbing down as carefully and quietly as possible. "I don't want to disturb any fairy things out there that we might not see," he whispered.

"Why did you put a bell in the trap?" asked Evelyn.

"I got to thinking," Reed said softly as he straightened out his clothes from the climb, "Tinker Bell was a fairy, and she liked bells, and do you remember when I looked all over for my space glider? One time when I looked under my bed, I saw a sparkle of light, and I remember that I heard a chime or a small bell. Maybe that was the fairy messing with me under my bed."

"Oh, Reed! I think you're making some connections that aren't really there. So you lost your space glider and found it later. I really think your imagination gets the best of you." Evelyn's retort was a little stinging, but Reed chose to ignore it.

"You do remember that my space glider disappeared and then reappeared before our very eyes, don't you?" Reed was excited as the two dashed back home.

"Do you really think you can attract a fairy?"

Reed answered, in a tone all too familiar to Evelyn, "I won't know unless I try."

"What's next?"

"We'll come back and check it tomorrow."

* * *

They returned the next day with much anticipation. Reed climbed the tree to find small twigs stuffed inside the opening of the trap and called down to Evelyn, trying not to be too loud, "The trap has some twigs inside beside the pine needles! I want whatever we catch to feel right at home. I'll look inside to see if there's anything there." He called down after inspecting and returning the trap, "There's nothing in there. Everything is just the way I left it." He felt as dejected as he sounded.

A big gust of wind blew over him as he descended, almost knocking him to the ground, but he held tightly to the branches. Evelyn screamed, as Reed was too high to fall and not be injured. He certainly didn't want to get in trouble with his parents, so he took additional care to be deliberate and cautious as he moved down the tree.

"We can come back tomorrow, and if nothing is trapped again, then I'll have to find out what else I can use as bait."

"Maybe a little more research is in order, and I can help you with that." Evelyn felt bad after all the work Reed had put into making the trap. He also had more glitter all over the back near his neck.

"Oh, Reed! You should see yourself. We'd better brush you off really, really well before Mom and Dad see you! You've got more glitter on your shoulders! At least it's not as much as before."

"What! Are you serious?" he asked in disbelief. Either he'd brushed up against something or there was a tiny something that had it out for him, he thought. "Hmph, I keep forgetting to be a lot more aware of what's going on around me so this doesn't happen. This stuff is the worst to get rid of!"

* * *

The next day was rainy, which suited the kids just fine, as they were determined to find information about proper bait for capturing fairies. For hours, they pored over a great many websites, but because the subject was considered imaginary, well, it was challenging.

Reed was a little disappointed. "I'm not sure how we'll catch that fairy. We both saw it; I even got another glimpse when it moved past me and warned us to get out of the pine forest."

"You may have to sit in the forest and wait and watch for a very long time, Reed. Do you have the patience for that?" asked Evelyn. She wasn't particularly interested or motivated to do the same, as she really wanted to return to the kitchen and experiment with baking new recipes.

Reed was quick to respond. "I may not have the patience, but I do have the motivation and the determination!"

"Well, then, I'll know where to find you if ever I'm looking! And I'll make sure to let Mom and Dad know in case they need you for something."

"Don't tell Mom and Dad *why* I'm in the forest. Just tell them I'm scouting for a possible fort site or that I'm making science notes."

"You got it. Just make sure not to get any more of that glitter stuff on you, or it won't take much for Mom and Dad to figure out where you were. I'm tired of helping you get that stuff off! Oh, and Reed, watch what you bring in on your shoes."

Reed went on to pack some creature comforts to make his pine woods visit comfortable. "I think I'm ready, Evelyn. I can't think of anything else that I need, and if there is some reason that I need to return home, then I'll pick up that stuff later. I think I'll take Rupert with me, so I'll bring a water dish for him."

Reed and Rupert hiked with fervent determination. Walking to the pine forest entrance that the family had used for the picnic, Reed wondered if the *Stay Out* message was still there. He looked down at where the warning was once displayed, but not a single small stick from the message was to be found. He entered the forest, expecting a big gust of wind like the one he had experienced before. Again, nothing. He continued on, looking for a suitable spot in the pine woods comfortable enough to establish a stakeout. Once settled, he sat and waited, looking the pine trees up and down, and then down and up. He could see the trap from where he'd established his stakeout about ten feet away; being a perfect distance was critical, as he didn't want to be so close that he'd make noise and be heard by the fairy, and he certainly did not want to be seen. With his eyes fixated on the trap, he sat petting Rupert for a while.

At first, Reed was glad that he had Rupert's companionship, but dogs don't stay still long unless they're very tired. Rupert did begin to snooze, but French bulldogs typically snore when they sleep, and when they're awake, they're well known for passing gas. Reed found both situations deterrents for viewing fairies, which left him regretting that he'd brought Rupert along. He decided he would return Rupert home if he wasn't quiet, but Rupert's snores settled down, and after two hours of watching the trap steadily, Reed began repeating to himself, "I will not get tired. I will not get tired." He was still very determined to return home with his capture, but he questioned how long he could endure the stakeout. He was only in fourth grade, after all.

He soon changed his message to "I'm going to succeed. I'm going to succeed." Doing this helped him feel able to sustain his watch, and after two more hours of patiently waiting, Reed had quietly snacked on his lunch and drank all his water, making sure Rupert stayed hydrated as well, although the noise of him lapping up water was sure to scare away any fairy. Halfway through the day, Reed again began questioning his plan. It was time for a break and a return home, where he would leave Rupert and grab his science observation notebook. Before going, he went up the tree to verify that the trap was still secure and the bait was still in the trap. Opening the trap slowly, he looked inside to find everything intact and unchanged. He sighed in disappointment and reminded himself that being patient would pay off.

After going home, he felt renewed, and he returned to his stakeout without too much time passing. Doodling absent-mindedly with a twig on the ground, he felt more bored than he had with Rupert earlier. "Oh no! I almost forgot to check the trap status!" He quickly climbed and checked to find nothing had changed and wondered whether or not to add something new to the trap. Then the thought of his mom's garden popped into his head. "I wonder if it would help if I offered the fairies a flower in the trap or maybe a sweet treat of Evelyn's making; I'm sure she wouldn't mind sharing."

His mind wandered as he waited, and he found himself having to repeatedly concentrate on watching the trap. A small wind blew through the trees, cooling him off as the day grew increasingly warmer. He needed more water, and he wondered if he should leave to get a refill and snack before the early-evening shift began. His steady gaze on the long pine branch ten feet above him gripped his attention. A lone pine needle floated slowly to the ground. Another needle fell, then another, until a large area of the branch was bare. Reed thought back to the staring contests he'd had with his friends in class and recalled staring so long and intensely on something that an inanimate object would appear to move. Is that what was happening now? Rubbing his eyes, he took another look in disbelief, then walked around the pine floor to wake himself up from the long day of guarding the stakeout post, all while fixing his gaze onto the branch's movement. Part of the branch formed a circular nest while falling needles floated to the nest's interior, as if to prepare for a tiny bed for the evening. The sky was beginning to darken, and Reed could hear his mother calling him home for the evening.

"I don't want to go home now. Things are just starting

to happen, or have I been standing at this outpost so long that I'm beginning to see things?" Speaking aloud to himself was enough to stop the unfurling of one of the small pine branches. He froze in his tracks, ignoring his mother's repeated calls. "I'm going to get in trouble if I don't go inside," he muttered under his breath, and he slowly headed back home but remembered to mark the spot where he wanted to return the next morning.

Once outside the pine forest, he picked up speed to share the day's events with Evelyn. Reaching the patio, he took a second to compose himself a little. "Oh, hi, Mom. Have you seen Evelyn?"

"What? Is that all I get? You've been gone all day. I'd like to hear how it went, especially since Evelyn said that you spent all your free hours in the forest!"

"Oh, well, I just basically staked out the forest to see what wildlife I would see there. I spent the entire day there because I wanted to see how the morning and the afternoon differ, which is why I plan on doing the same tomorrow. Besides, we always have a paper to write when we go back to school about what we did during the summer, and I can use this day and our picnic when I describe this awesome forest. Oh, and I'm sure I can use the information from this time in the pine woods for some future science project. That's why I need to be in the forest for a long time–to compare before-and-after data. Hey, Mom! Can I use the camera tomorrow?"

Brilliant, Reed, he thought. Catching some of those unbelievable moments on camera would be a big help in solving these mysterious happenings! *Maybe I'll catch the branch waving or forming a tiny nest. Or maybe I'll capture one of those tiny bugs that look like they have human faces. I might even find out where the glitter is coming from; the ultimate would be a picture of a fairy itself!* He felt reenergized at the prospects.

"Yes, you can use the camera, but it's expensive, and if you cause any damage, you'll have to work off the cost of fixing it. Are you prepared to do that? And what do you want the camera for?"

"I want to get some nature pictures for my science notebook. You can count on me to take extra special care. I promise!"

"Evelyn!" he called as he ran upstairs to get the camera.

Perusing a couple cookbooks, Evelyn looked up as Reed passed her room. "Hi, Reed. Where are you going with the camera?"

He quickly did an about-face in the hallway to address her. "Wow, you've got to listen to this! To be honest, I wasn't totally sure that I could sit in the forest the entire day. At first it was pretty boring, and I really thought I wouldn't see a thing, and maybe I was wasting my time. I set the trap very carefully, and you remember that I put one of those little bells with glitter inside again."

"Did you trap anything?"

"No, I checked." Reed's disappointment was clear. "I didn't see much until right before I got ready to leave." He settled himself with a pillow on the floor. "It was getting to be twilight, so it was hard to see clearly, but I sat and stared at this pine branch, and I noticed that it was starting to lose some of its needles, and then the branch started to change its shape entirely. I just couldn't take my eyes off it. Certainly, whatever was happening was making a nest of some kind. I couldn't believe what I saw! That's why tomorrow I'm bringing a camera to catch some of this stuff on film. I really wish you could come with me, but I know that you wouldn't want to sit there all day; you're too busy."

"You go out to the forest tomorrow with the camera, and if you're able to see anything unusual there, I'll see it on the pictures that you take."

"All right." Reed was disappointed that he wouldn't have Evelyn's company but he was thrilled with his idea to bring a camera. He took his pencil and paper to create a list of what to pack for the next day of Operation Stakeout, and he wondered how many days of waiting he would have to endure until something significant happened again.

Prisoner Plans

I know that if I can take a picture of something, it'll be worth the wait, Reed thought as he replayed the days' spectacular events over and over again in his mind.

* * *

Shaking the picnic blanket free from leftover crumbs, Reed gathered an extra water bottle, bug spray, film, the camera, and a couple of snacks. The weather looked like rain, so he wanted to be prepared by bringing a raincoat just in case, and he reminded his mother before he left home that he knew enough to watch for threatening weather and he promised to come home if the weather looked at all serious.

He set out early, leaving Rupert behind to ensure fewer distractions in the forest. After a short search, Reed found the area he had marked the day before. He rechecked that the camera contained film as his anticipation mounted. Hours of waiting made the day look very much like the day before, except today, a bit of cooling light rain fell. Reed was grateful for it. He could feel the protection the pines offered from the covering of the canopy above, and the pine floor would stay fairly dry since it wasn't raining hard. The air felt humid, warm, and thick, but he was determined to stay ready to capture anything unusual on film. An ant carrying pieces of dirt large for its size to a small hole at the bottom of a tree captured his attention for some time. Soon there were several ants doing the same, and before long, Reed saw an army of ants moving in and out of the hole systematically. About two feet above the hole, a large, winged insect with a distorted face hovered next to the tree. It eerily passed as a human face but was had enormous fly-like eyes. Antennae emerged from its head with small tufts of hair on either side. The fluttering insect held a clipboard on which it was taking notes on the coming and goings of the ants below.

Reed sat so enthralled watching the ants work that he hadn't thought of taking his camera out to photograph the unusual work director that fluttered before him. Reed wondered what the construction below the tree might look like with such a flurry of activity. He heard barely audible musical notes, which he at first thought were the flapping of the bug's wings or the orchestrated ant movement, but listening further, he looked higher up the tree to find a ray of light shining upon some movement on the branches, as if to highlight a momentous act about to unfold. He couldn't utter a sound but sat captivated to see what was about to emerge from the highlighted branch.

Beneath it, a very small stalk emerged and began splitting away from the larger branch. Lime green in color, the new, smaller section of wood unfurled into what looked like a tiny new branch, but transformed by stretching out transparent wings alongside an extended body. A newborn bundle with needles along the trunk of the dark green body fell to the wayside, and a long stream of ants each connected to form a bridge to hold the newborn and prevent it from falling. They moved closer to the small nest that had been unfurled earlier on the tree branch.

Reed had never seen such a sight before. New life had developed before his eyes, and he wasn't even sure what kind of newborn the fledgling might be. The director of the ants, below, signaled to the group of workers to return beneath the tree and was followed by the entrance of several small, winged creatures. They quickly flew to the nest, singing, with a luminescent aura about them, not noticing the fixed gaze steadily watching them. The creatures were entirely focused on the newborn in their presence and sang to it to comfort and soothe it while they encircled it.

Reed wanted so badly to get closer to see what the minute beings were doing or saying to the newborn, but he knew that if he were disruptive, he would surely scare the creatures away. Just then, the small fluttering creatures flew away from the newborn as if to allow Reed and the world a peek at the new being that would evolve further from a light green to a dark green color, then to a beautiful, pale rainbow of fluorescent colors. Reed thought the brightness of the baby's coloring would surely attract predators of some sort, but the winged creatures whisked the newborn up so quickly, Reed saw only the nest left behind, and it soon fell to the ground to became food for the ants below.

Realizing that his opportunity to take a picture was almost completely gone, Reed grabbed his camera and thought at the very last second to photograph the pile of ants working on the leftover broken nest that had fallen. *Click*. A flash of light signaled to the ants to scurry away, leaving a deserted site behind.

"Wow! There's nothing left of the nest, and the ants are all gone—every last one of them! Those had to be fairies I saw. They were just beautiful!"

Quietly gathering his camera and lens cap, Reed messed up the area he had used to observe so as not to leave evidence that he had been there, in case the fairies

returned. He hurried home with so many unanswered questions to talk to Evelyn about and sort through.

Swiftly opening the back patio door to the kitchen, Reed blurted breathlessly, "Evelyn! You won't believe what I just saw." He could hardly get his words out fast enough.

In his excitement, he'd forgotten to check the trap and recalled that he had wanted to add a couple of more appealing items to it in hopes of enticing a fairy, although he wasn't so sure that he wanted to capture a fairy anymore. They were such stunning creatures, and with the ability to use magical powers, Reed desperately want to avoid getting on their bad side, especially since he felt he might have overstepped his bounds and infringed upon their habitat.

"Where were you, Reed? I called out looking for you, but you didn't answer."

"I was staked out in the forest, and I'm sorry that I didn't come home right away, sis, but I was watching the most amazing sight in the pine trees!" Reed adjusted the kitchen chair to get comfortable as he continued. "First, I found what I thought was a great viewing spot on the blanket, and then I sat watching the trap and the area around it. It was getting a little boring not seeing anything go in or out of the trap, but I tried really hard to not to take my eyes off it."

He continued while Evelyn readied another dessert for the oven. "Then I started to watch this ant colony go into and out of a hole at the bottom of this pine tree. Super interesting to watch, but they were so busy that I almost didn't notice an extremely large bug flying above the ants. I could've sworn I saw little glasses on its face while it held a small clipboard. It sort of looked . . . hmm, like Uncle Ben–Mom's brother–more than a bug! It had large eyes like a fly does, and . . ." Reed paused at the thought. "Can you imagine a bug with hair? It looked like there was actual hair on top of its head!"

Evelyn was enthralled. She sat down, watching Reed relay the story of his afternoon spent in the pine woods. "Did the bug look like it would hurt you?"

"No. I mean, I didn't see a stinger or anything. It just hovered in one spot over the ants while it kept looking down. It looked as if it were giving directions to the ants, but I couldn't tell what it was saying. All I heard was some kind of insect-speak, and then all the ants went into the hole very fast, and before I knew it, they all disappeared underground."

Evelyn skeptically listened to every word. Could Reed be making all of this up? "So what happened next?" she asked, trying instead to be supportive.

"Then I watched this tree branch lose a bunch of

needles, but it was only one section of the branch that lost them, and each needle fell down to the ground slowly, and then"–Reed stood with his arms raising higher, his hands turning as if to support something small–"this nest started to form out of nowhere!"

Evelyn tried to comprehend what sounded like a bunch of nonsense. "You're saying that a nest magically formed from the pine needles that fell? That's certainly an incredible story!" She was working hard to believe him, and she thought back to the strange things that had been happening since they had moved in, resigned to the possibility that he was telling her the truth.

"Evelyn, the nest just wondrously assembled itself. Listen, I can hardly believe any of this happened myself. I just wanted to tell you the details before I forgot. Hey, do you remember those pictures of fairies on the Internet? Well, I really think we found the real deal. These fairies flew near the nest, I guess, to watch over it. They kind of glowed, and they had some kind of halos around their heads. They were very pretty. Nope–I'd actually use the word *beautiful*, not *pretty*. And they made this real faint musical noise, but you have to listen very closely. I thought I'd heard them another time when I entered the forest, but I wasn't sure what it was at the time. Now I know!"

"Wow, Reed. That's some story." They went to their

rooms to finish their conversation before their parents came home.

"Except it's not a story. I did forget to look in the trap today, but I'm not sure that I still want to capture a fairy or anything else in a trap. I did get a picture of something. Let me tell you about the best part of the story. After the nest was formed, I think the fairies had a baby! This branch sort of shed another branch, and the ants formed a long ladder from it."

Evelyn was beginning to think Reed sounded ridiculous. "I thought you said that the ants went into a hole."

"They did, but they must have had a way up the tree or there were more ants up on the branch that I didn't see earlier." He didn't care if Evelyn believed his entire story; he knew what he'd seen and that he hadn't imagined a thing. "The ants made a sort of bridge, and they carried what I think was a baby fairy to the nest. Boy, it was super cool! I've never seen anything like this before! At first, the baby sort of looked like a tiny, narrow, bright green stick with little bitty wings on either side of it. I wish you could've seen it!" He sounded as if he had just struck gold. It was a little hard for him to put his finger on what he was feeling. He could hardly believe what he had just witnessed in the woods, and he was at a loss for any other explanation.

"I suppose if I joined you in the woods tomorrow, I wouldn't see any of those fairies or any of the ants." Evelyn was disappointed that she had missed the opportunity to see the spectacle Reed had just described, and she couldn't help but feel a little left out of the fun and excitement. She opted to take the high road and not share her envious feelings, turning them into excitement for Reed.

"I'm sure they wouldn't be at that exact spot tomorrow, because I may have scared them away, but if we waited long enough, who knows what we might see, Evelyn! I think that's the key—be patient and make it seem like you're just part of the forest yourself."

"How long do you think we'll have to wait?"

"However long it takes for any pine forest creature to feel safe enough to come out of the woodwork, I guess." Reed chuckled. "Pun intended."

"Well, when do you think we can go back so that I can see for myself?"

"I'd be happy to take you to the spot as soon as I've got some free time. First, I want to look up more information; my mind is going in so many different directions. I had better figure out what I just saw."

"Good idea. It's always best to do that before you forget any of the facts."

"If we can find out more about the life of a fairy, we might be able to figure out the best time of day to see these creatures. I also wonder about their life cycle–kind of like we had to read on the life cycle of frogs. If we get more facts on these buggers, then we might learn something that we can use. Knowledge is power, you know. Oh! I did manage to take a picture of the last bits of the very cool moment that I saw today in the pines."

"You'll want to get those developed right away, and when you do, we'll have to keep them in a very safe place."

"I completely agree!" Reed looked at some information on his computer. "It says here that the word *sprite* comes from the Latin for *spirit* and that fairies have a small, humanlike appearance, whereas pixies are smaller and more elfish."

"Pixies? Let me see. Is there a picture?" Evelyn's curiosity grew.

"No, but look, it says here that pixies are also typically found to be naughty. Hmm, they're the ones who got glitter all over me." He thought back to some of the perplexities of the past few weeks. "What do you think about making a list of all the weird things that took place over the last couple of weeks?"

"Not a bad idea."

"We might make some connections between all the weird stuff that I just saw in the forest and what's been happening around here that we've had a hard time explaining. It couldn't hurt. Besides those times that I was glittered, what else happened that we thought was weird or that we couldn't explain?"

It didn't take long for Evelyn to think back to the egg that had mysteriously cracked itself into her cake batter or to the chime and glimmer of light that Reed had found under his bed when looking for his space glider.

"Don't forget the cakes being frosted by themselves and the mug that was broken and reassembled," Evelyn added.

"What about that warning we saw in the sticks just before we went into the pine woods for the picnic? We'll want to add that to our list." Reed paused, looking up from his notes. "What about Mom and Dad? Shouldn't we tell them what we've been doing?"

Evelyn looked at Reed seriously. "I don't know why we'd have to mention anything to them. I'm also not sure if those creatures in the woods have been in our house. How would they get here, and what purpose would they have to be in our house?" The thought spooked Evelyn. "We haven't seen any of them around here. Do they appear and disappear at will, or do they move so quickly that we don't see them?"

"Those are just a couple of questions on a long list of others I have!"

Evelyn searched the room for anything unusual, and her mind started swimming, not knowing what to even call those creatures, much less how to explain the house mysteries of late. "I think we should be careful who we blame for the strange things going on around here. For example, if the chain on my necklace broke, I don't want to blame someone or something; they might want to retaliate against us."

"I know. I thought about that, too," Reed said. "One moment I'm all ready to trap one of those things, and then I'm afraid to. I'm totally unsure of whether it's a good idea or not."

"I think we should go ahead with the trap and just keep on monitoring it and adjusting the bait. You never know what we might find in there. Who knows? Maybe something will happen when we're in the woods. Also, keep taking notes; there may be some clue that could help us find out more."

"Have you ever heard that saying 'Luck is preparation meeting opportunity?'" Reed pondered over those words. "I heard that somewhere, and I really believe that. All the time we've spent researching will pay off. I *really, really* hope, with all my heart, we'll find the answer in my trap—and soon. And after we've got answers to these mysteries, we can set whatever we've trapped free."

5.

Small but Mighty Warnings

While days passed and Reed spent all his spare time researching fairy life, Evelyn continued baking different desserts to enter in the upcoming county fair. She grew even more confident in her skills and became exceedingly masterful at baking bread, although those particular recipes were time consuming, and the bread got stale quickly. She had a knack for embellishing a standard recipe, lifting it up to make something worthy of high praise, which she soaked up proudly.

She took days to search through her many recipes filed

in cookbooks and three-ring binders. Setting aside a half dozen, she settled on preparing the one she felt most confident would win the top purple ribbon at the fair. She'd chosen her grandmother's Norwegian apple pastry cake, a fairly straightforward recipe but one unique enough to be noticed and delicious enough to be remembered for a long time, she hoped. She knew that simple was often better than complex and that this recipe wasn't very difficult, although most kids her age would be challenged by it. She only had to worry about not overworking the crust, and she wanted an assortment of apples for a more well-rounded flavor so the judges wouldn't find the cake overly sweet or too tart. She had found that a blend of apples–Galas, Granny Smiths, and Pink Ladies–was the winning combination for her county fair recipe.

She made sure to use local apples as much as possible, too–her grandmother's advice through the years for her cake to contain optimal flavor. Evelyn thought back to a family trip to Mexico where she'd tasted the most amazingly sweet orange. She'd learned from her grandmother and school that when food is allowed to ripen fully, it soaks up nutrients from the sun and ground completely, making it fully flavorful. "That's why strawberries taste like cardboard here in the Midwest during winter, Evelyn," her grandmother used to tell her. Late summer was the perfect time for apples, so Evelyn felt certain about her recipe choice.

Additionally, she knew to carefully weigh each ingredient so that she could be as accurate as possible. She also needed to make two cakes so she could pick the best for her fair entry. She painstakingly assembled her ingredients, informing Reed that *mise en place*, or the organization of a recipe's ingredients, was important so that she would not forget an ingredient or step, and after the earlier egg episode, she wanted to use the utmost care. Continuing to check the directions to her recipe so that she didn't overlook a step, she completed the assembly, put the cakes in the oven, and set the timer. She double-checked the wall clock over the oven to see what time she should remove her baked goodies, but she noticed that it wasn't working; it read 12:00 when it was still very early in the morning. She removed the wall clock and set it to the correct current time of 9:23, and then replaced it on the wall.

"Okay, Rupert, I've got a little time before my pastry cakes are done! Let's go check on Reed and see what he's up to." Finding Reed packing, Evelyn inquired, "What's on your agenda for the day?"

"I'm getting ready for more stakeout time in the pine woods. Want to come with?"

"I have a couple of cakes in the oven now. What time

were you thinking of heading out to the site?"

"Right after lunch. I'm not finding too much information on the Internet about fairies, and I thought I might try putting some new stuff in the trap."

"What bait are you thinking to put in the trap now?" Evelyn didn't have much faith in her brother's ability to catch a fairy–or much else, for that matter.

Reed walked back into the kitchen with Evelyn following. His eyes wandered over the counter space to the sink to gather a clue about what Evelyn's mighty oven held as its heat transformed the ingredients inside. "I thought I might get a tiny bit of something that you recently created in the kitchen."

"Hmm. Well, I am making a couple of apple pie cakes. You can have a small slice from the one that I don't enter into the county fair."

"Is it a pastry or a cake?"

"Actually, it's one and the same. It's Grandma's recipe– it's called a *pastry cake* because it's baked like a cake and it has this delicious vanilla sauce that bakes with the apples."

"Thanks, Evvie. But I really need some larger crumbs. Maybe I'll just take a tiny bit of one of your cookies in the cookie jar. When is the county fair?" He snipped a large cookie crumb to save for the trap in a small plastic bag.

"Next week."

"Won't your pastry cake be stale by then if you're baking it now?"

"It'll go into the freezer, silly. I want the cake to be perfect, so once it cools off, I'll wrap it tightly to keep it fresh and freeze it. Of course, it has to come out of the oven looking and tasting like I think a purple ribbon Norwegian apple pastry cake should look and taste. Grandma would have had several purple ribbons if she had entered any number of her baked goods into the fair." The Norwegian apple pastry cake had been a family recipe for years, so Evelyn was very hopeful that it would be as much of a hit among the fair judges as it had been with her family. "I still have about another half hour before they're done baking."

"Do you ever stop to wonder what we're doing? I mean, I'm carrying a small plastic bag with a tiny bit of cookie in hopes that I can trap a fairy! That sounds unbelievable! Hey, I sure hope that you don't tell anyone about this. People will think I'm making stuff up and they won't take me seriously–especially since we're about to attend a new school soon. I want to make new friends, and if they think I'm weird in any way, then they won't stay friends for long!"

"I understand, Reed. I'm in the same boat."

Before long, Evelyn opened the oven door to take out the cakes, surveying each one to determine which might be a contender for the fair. Her eyes opened widely, and her mouth dropped. "Oh no, Reed! I've made this cake before with excellent results, but look at it now! It looks like the apples sank to the bottom before baking together with the vanilla sauce. I can't enter either of these in the county fair!" Both cakes' interiors had a separated apple-and-vanilla-sauce center when they should have combined as they baked. "I'll have to ask Mom when she gets home what she wants done with these cakes. I know they'll taste just fine, but the fair judges don't judge on the flavor alone. These cakes would definitely not be ribbon-worthy!"

She set the cakes on the stove to cool and dejectedly left to walk the now very familiar pine forest route with Reed, hoping to take her mind off her cake disaster. They set out with only a couple of hours to spend in the woods, the air very still, bordering on stifling. Looking down at the water bottles that she carried, she was happy she remembered to bring them.

Evelyn noticed the path to the woods was becoming more defined as the grass and weeds wore away. The distance seemed shorter to Reed after making the same route time and time again. Upon entering the woods, Reed pointed ahead to show Evelyn where he had witnessed the fairy birth days before. They looked up and around to see if they noticed anything out of the ordinary. Moving quietly, they tried not to attract attention, Evelyn following Reed and not uttering a word. Soon Reed pointed to the tree that contained the nest and the ant hole. Looking down at the bottom of the tree, there was not a single ant near it or any evidence of any branch missing needles where the nest had been. Reed searched other trees, carefully assessing whether that tree was the one where he'd remembered the strange events taking place. He looked at his science notebook, where he had written a detailed description.

He looked at Evelyn with the same disappointment she had displayed a short time earlier. "I don't understand this! I know this is the tree that had the nest and this is the spot on the branch where the nest rested. Even if I'm wrong, there are only two or three other trees in this area where the birth could've taken place, because these are the only trees that have the same kind of lower branches I saw being used as the baby fairy's nest."

"Why don't we plant ourselves down in a couple of different spots and see if anything happens while we wait?" Evelyn's frustration with her cakes had disappeared, and she could easily empathize with Reed. She tried to be encouraging. "You said that you had waited quite a while before anything took place yesterday."

"I suppose you're right. Waiting for such a long time

gets so boring." Reed tried to overcome his disappointment. "Hey, why don't I climb up and check out that trap? I brought a small bit of cookie to put inside."

"Good idea." Evelyn watched him climb the tree and hoped that he would be pleasantly surprised. Reed was back down to the forest floor before she knew it, but she knew by the look on his face that nothing new had happened in the trap. Before he could say anything, Evelyn reminded him, "Remember, Mom and Dad always tell us, 'Good things come to those who wait.' Or maybe the fairies are just not trap-able."

"I didn't really think of that. Maybe I should think outside the box—or trap, as the case may be." Reed smiled at his own play on words. He looked around the immediate area to find spaces suitable for each of them to rest for a while. Of course, the optimal viewing area for a possible fairy spotting had to be comfortable, and they wanted to be within earshot of each other just in case they had to communicate.

Evelyn made herself as comfortable as possible, using her best posture, sitting cross-legged on her picnic blanket. She balled up a sweater she had brought to lean on in the unlikely event that the weather got much cooler, and she set her focus straight ahead, viewing each tree before her, from left to right, up and down, and very systematically for the possibility of an unusual sighting.

Reed took a little longer to get settled but had pretty much set his old sweatshirt down, with his water bottle and snack bag in the exact same positions as when he'd viewed the fairy the first time. He tried to replicate as many of the previous conditions as possible, because he so wanted it to happen again–partly because it was spectacular but also because he wanted Evelyn to see it.

They waited and waited and waited some more. With probably more patience than most kids their age, they enjoyed taking in the view around them and listening to the various movements of birds and animals in the outer areas of the woods. To amuse themselves and to pass the time, they began throwing a small twig to each other without being too distracting.

The pine tree shadows had shifted enough that Evelyn looked at her watch. She motioned to Reed that it was time to get back home. He reluctantly obliged and packed up his belongings while trying to get one last look around, just in case something happened. They returned to the path just out of the forest when the wind picked up again, swaying the pine trees so hard that older pine needles began falling at a rapid pace. Evelyn could see the grassy field just beyond the forest standing perfectly still in contrast to the boisterous wind that blew around them within the woods. She thought this strong wind must be the type to break trees, so she gestured to Reed to hurry but also pointed to the contrasting field just outside the forest area that remained calm.

Reed tried to speak above the noise, enunciating his words for Evelyn to hear. "Yes, I can see the field. What's going on? There doesn't seem to be any wind blowing over there!"

Before they could exit the pines, a small, fluorescent, glowing ball rolled before them at eye level. Evelyn and Reed stopped in their tracks, shaking as the ball floated for a few moments. The levitating ball seemed to open on the side that faced them with the lifting of a small wall. A very decorated and clearly high-ranking official fairy sat hovering just inside the glowing ball on a throne as he stared down at the children. His arms were crossed with authority, his anger obvious, and his voice was small but loud enough for them to hear him clearly. No fear could be detected on his face.

Evelyn and Reed were stunned, not knowing what to do or say. They stared at the fairy and listened.

"I am the honorable fairy magistrate. You will address me as Your Honor or Ashkin. I have been forced to enlighten you humans because you have returned once again to violate our beautiful pine forest. You have been given a sign to stay out of our property, but you've chosen to ignore it. Furthermore, you have unforgivably trampled upon and disturbed our holy worship area. We have cursed you with glitter, and still you chose to return. And the vilest of offenses . . ." The fairy magistrate paused to make himself very clear. "Well, that is the witness of our private and beloved clan baby's birth. Those who witness such a sacred occasion are invited, which you were not. We will be forced to enter your domain and make your life progressively worse if you continue to ignore our warnings. These will not be simple warnings, you see, if you continue to violate our land; they will be hurtful, defensive tactics that we are most certain will deter you from entering our beautiful pine home. If you choose to obey and stay far away, your life will be uplifted, and you will be bestowed favors of kindness and gestures to enrich your lives. You make the choice!" Ashkin was a small but mighty fairy.

"Um, uh . . . Yes, of course, Your Honor—I mean, Ashkin," Evelyn said, her voice growing louder as she spoke. She couldn't help but want to whisper, but she also wanted to show respect. "My brother and I certainly don't mean you any harm." She tried to speak clearly, but her voice was very shaky as she stood there trembling. Her grip on Reed's hand tightened significantly, too shocked to even move as her topsy-turvy mind tried to process this small but mighty creature before them.

"Go on your way, then, but heed my warning–or else!" The front wall closed, and the fairy's sphere floated away.

Evelyn and Reed just stood there, watching the ball of flame disappear in the distance.

"See, I told you I wasn't joking. They really do exist! I told you! I told you." Reed's fear subsided, and his excitement built.

"Wow, Reed," Evelyn stumbled, trying to sort out her thoughts. "I really didn't think that you were lying about the fairies, but I guess I did think you were stretching the truth. This explains so much! Think about it . . ."

They began to walk home at a quickening pace, holding their conversation while looking around to see if there was any view of the fireball they had just witnessed.

"That was bizarre . . . and a little scary!"

"See, I told you that if we waited around long enough . . ." Reed shut the patio door behind them.

"I know some of the things going on around here have been very weird–I wonder if the fairies are behind all of it."

"I wonder, too, but remember what Ashkin just told us. He said that they will make life difficult and progressively worse."

Stopping in her tracks, Evelyn reached out to stop Reed from moving. "Reed, look! My cakes! Do you remember how my cakes had fallen and the batter was a mess? Look at them! They're beautiful! Wow!" She was breathless at how this cake disaster could look so picture-perfect. "I have no idea how they rose again. I was so disappointed in how they'd collapsed before we went outside."

She searched the kitchen and opened the fridge, where there was only a partially eaten cake from the other day, then opened both the top and bottom oven doors to make certain there were no cakes there. Glancing on the kitchen table and along the kitchen counters, she saw there was no sight of her two Norwegian cakes that had flopped.

"What happened? You did see that both cakes looked terrible when I took them out of the oven, and you know how badly I felt about them before we went to the forest." Before Reed could answer, a thought entered her mind. "Do you think that Ashkin fixed my cakes because we left the forest right away?"

Reed was at a loss for any other explanation. Evelyn washed her hands before removing the cakes from the springform pans, carefully setting each one on a plate. She analyzed them to determine which one she would enter into the county fair and which one would be used to taste test.

The children shared a small piece to test its baking success. Reed gobbled his bit of cake down, while Evelyn chose to hold her piece of cake high, looking carefully at the its texture and the flakiness of its crust, double-checking its color, and finally taking a bite to see if the cake was, indeed, fair-worthy.

"I don't taste anything at all wrong with the flavor. Well, I might not have an explanation for why it went from disaster to picture-worthy, but I now have a cake that I think stands a strong chance of earning a very worthy ribbon." After wrapping both cakes carefully to preserve their freshness, she put the cake destined for the county fair into the freezer. "That reminds me, Reed, don't forget to give Mom and Dad the film to get those pictures developed so we can see what you captured in the woods."

"Thanks; I'll ask Dad tonight. Should I take some photos of your cakes to use up the film?"

"I don't care, but I'm not sure we should go back to the woods."

"I'm with you for now."

Hungry, she wanted a late lunch, as she had eaten just a small snack in the forest. She checked the time and saw that the clock she had adjusted earlier that morning now read 8:45. She knew that the time was once again incorrect, but she wasn't sure how much time she and Reed had spent in the forest, so she checked the living room anniversary clock. That clock read 3:15.

"Hmm, what's wrong with our clocks?" she asked herself. Still not convinced that the living room clock was correct, she went to her bedroom to find her watch, which rested on her dresser. That time read 9:21. "What's going on? So far, there haven't been two clocks in this house that have had the same time."

Frustrated, she turned on the radio, which announced the time and temperature regularly. She wiped up the crumbs from the counter as she heard the radio announcer state the current time of 2:15. She walked directly to the kitchen clock and set it for the second time that day, then reset the other clocks. She then went to Reed's room, where he was writing in a small notebook. He looked up from his desk.

"Reed, do you have a watch or clock in your room?"

"Yes, I have both. Why?"

"What time do they have?"

He took out his watch from his desk drawer. "My watch says 5:17." He immediately looked up at Evelyn, knowing quite well it was not 5:17. He reached over to view his alarm clock. "Look, my alarm clock says 7:33. Hey, what's up with that? I used my watch yesterday, and it was working just fine then, and my alarm clock was working this morning."

"I wonder if that fairy magistrate changed all the

clocks in our house, although I didn't get the feeling he was the type to play such petty tricks. I looked at several different clocks just now, and they all had different times." She contemplated the latest mix-ups. "It certainly would explain a lot of things around here. What if we offer that fairy magistrate a gift so he won't be mad at us? Then maybe these pranks the fairies are playing on us might stop. Who knows? They might be even nicer and more helpful to us."

"What in the world would a fairy like for a gift?" He wasn't sure if a present was the answer to solving all their problems, especially since there had been no results with his fairy-trapping idea. Meanwhile, he went to his computer, this time to research what they could offer Ashkin.

"I'll think it over, but right now, I've got to get back to the kitchen and get those cake dishes in the dishwasher."

Heavily in thought about the earlier warning from Ashkin, she entered the kitchen and approached the sink. She looked around for the bowls, measuring cups, and spoons she had used to make the Norwegian apple pastry cakes. Opening the dishwasher, she thought she might have absent-mindedly loaded it earlier, but the dishwasher only held the used morning breakfast dishes. "Hmm," she muttered under her breath as she walked around to the pantry to return the flour. There she spotted a dish towel spread on the counter, neatly arranged with all the dishes she'd used earlier.

"What's happening here? I definitely didn't put those dishes there." She knew that Reed hadn't washed the dishes; he had gone directly to his room when they'd returned from the pine forest. Maybe her parents were home early from work. Finding the garage empty, she texted her mother. She had been at work all day and texted back that she hadn't had time to come home and their father had meetings scheduled throughout the day.

She called out, "Reed, come down here quickly! I've got to show you something!"

Reed dashed down to the pantry. "What is it?"

"When I came downstairs to deal with the dirty dishes, they weren't in the sink where I had left them, and they weren't in the dishwasher either. When I went to the pantry, I found the dirty dishes were clean and very neatly arranged. I thought Mom or Dad came home early, so I checked with Mom but they've been at work. Did you tackle those dishes? Although I'm sure that I already know how you're going to answer."

Reed shook his head and rolled his eyes. "You know I hate doing dishes. I'd like to help you out, but I've been too busy looking for a peace offering to give Ashkin."

"Do you think a fairy did this?"

"If they can do things to mess up our lives, I suppose they can do things to be helpful."

Reed makes a lot of sense sometimes for a fourth grader, Evelyn thought. "Yeah, I suppose you're right, but I'm a little afraid of the not-so-nice things the fairies can do to us. Let's think a little harder about what to do or say to turn Ashkin's opinion of us around. I don't need to start a new school year with problems from him, and neither do you!"

"Agreed," Reed replied wholeheartedly. "I want to tell you something else that I've been thinking about. Do you think there's been one fairy or several hanging around our house? I really wonder a lot about the fairies—so much so that I should write my questions down."

"I know. I feel the same way, but I've got to get back to my prep work for the county fair. I want everything to be perfect for the entry, so I need to focus my attention on the details of my presentation for now."

6.

Questionable Judgment

The sunlight poured onto the kitchen counter as if it were shining a spotlight on Evelyn's county fair cake entry. She had been working for weeks to find the ultimate balance of sweet and tart apple flavors. Judgment day had finally arrived. Mrs. Gunderson took the day off from work so she could accompany Evelyn to the fair in the morning and then take the kids for school supplies and clothes that afternoon.

Their trip to the fairgrounds would be quick, as the crowds would arrive during the upcoming weekend.

Judging took place before the fair opened to the public. With her stomach churning, Evelyn watched the steady stream of baking entrants arrive into the culinary arts hall, each carrying a covered baked good in a variety of shapes, textures, and sizes. Some held quite elaborate tiers of frosted cake, while others brought more simple pies, breads, or cookies. She couldn't help but check over her shoulder at the various entries made with varying levels of ability–partly because she wanted to catch a view of her competition and partly because she feared Ashkin or another fairy might do something to sabotage her chances of placing highly. She sat on a cold aluminum chair next to her mother and held her cake proudly on her lap while she waited for the judge to call her over to the judging table.

Minutes seemed like hours until, finally, she was called. A very cheerful, rather stout lady extended her chubby arm toward Evelyn. "Hello, young lady. I am Mrs. Winston. Won't you set your lovely pastry down on the table, and we'll get to judging? Have a seat, won't you?" She motioned for Evelyn and her mother to sit in the chairs next to her judging table while she cut a piece of Evelyn's Norwegian apple pastry cake. "Tell me about your entry, Evelyn." Mrs. Winston looked at her notes.

Evelyn handed Mrs. Winston the judging sheet that she had been given. As Evelyn began talking, the judge took notes, analyzing the cake from all sides, checking the flakiness of the crust with a fork and poking around the pile of baked apples and the vanilla sauce enveloping each slice of fruit. Mrs. Winston took a large sniff, then a big bite while looking up—Evelyn supposed it was to not be distracted as she fully tasted the pastry cake. She jotted down a few more notes and let out a small squeal as she swallowed.

"Mmmm, that is exceedingly delicious, Evelyn! What did you say was in your cake?" Mrs. Winston read the recipe while listening to Evelyn rattle off the ingredients and the steps she'd taken to make the dessert.

As the judge added up the points, then recalculated, and recalculated a third time, Evelyn worried in the chair, obediently waiting. Her eyes fixated on Mrs. Winston, who reached into her box containing ribbons and made the selection under wraps, holding her hands and the ribbon below the table. She looked very sternly at Evelyn.

"I'm still a little confused, as there seems to be another flavor in this dessert that I can't quite put my finger on, but your pastry entry is exquisite. It has just the perfect flakiness and balance of sweetness to the apples. It's also a very unique dessert, being both a cake and a pie. Evelyn, I am awarding you a purple ribbon, as I've never tasted an entry quite this delicious and made with such high quality. I'll admit I thought I had seen perfect pie and cake recipes in the past, but yours is simply amazing!"

Evelyn's eyes opened widely while she reached over to receive the ribbon for her cake. Looking toward her mother, Evelyn gleamed with pride as she held the ribbon close to her heart.

"Unfortunately," Mrs. Winston continued, "I will need to take this ribbon back."

Evelyn was shocked.

"You see, my dear, we need to display your dessert in the display case, and your ribbon will be posted right next to it. You can pick up your dessert and ribbon when the fair concludes a week from Monday morning."

Evelyn looked at her mom with relief. As the two left, she noticed the judge take the cake over to another judge and hand her a taste. Evelyn watched the second judge's eyes grow wide in amazement, then smile and run to share it with yet another fair official. It was evident to Evelyn that she had hit a home run, but even she didn't know her entry was that glorious.

"I'm so thrilled, Mom! I can't wait to tell Dad about this!" Evelyn caught a glimpse of what she thought was a fairy quickly darting off a light high above and just behind her mom. It fluttered in the same position just long enough for Evelyn to see that the fairy was beautiful and female. She also caught the fairy giving her a thumbs-up.

"Evelyn, I'm so very proud of you. Let's go pick up Reed, and you can tell him all about it over lunch. I'll treat you both to some school shopping this afternoon, and we'll pick up the pictures from the store, too."

The two picked up Reed from his friend's house and Mrs. Gunderson said proudly, "Reed, Evelyn has good news to share with you!" Evelyn chose to sit in the back with Reed while their mother drove. After telling Reed about her placing, she motioned to him that she'd had another fairy sighting. Reed motioned back that he did as well. They couldn't wait to get back home to discuss their experiences without their mom listening in on their conversation.

* * *

After a whirlwind afternoon of purchasing new school supplies and clothes, Evelyn entered Reed's room and sat at his desk chair. "You tell me your news first, Reed. What sort of fairy encounter did you have?"

"I'm not completely sure, Ev. I was playing fetch with Rupert before I left this morning, and then we were wandering around looking into the edge of the yard. I saw Rupert sniffing the ground and digging a hole in the dirt as if he wanted to dig something up. I knew Mom wouldn't be happy with his dirty paws coming into the house, so

I tried to see what he was getting at. When I went to see what it was, well, you won't believe it!"

He removed a shoebox from his closet and carefully handed it to Evelyn. "Look in here, but don't get grossed out." She looked at him and slowly lifted the box's lid off, finding Reed had lined the bottom with tissue and cotton. Lying on top was the fragile skeleton of a fairy, with four large segments of wings still intact but tattered. Evelyn's eyebrows rose in shock. She studied the figure from top to bottom. "Reed! This is awesome, but there is no way Rupert dug this up and then you put it back together in the time before you went to your friend's house."

"No, Rupert was digging, all right. I had to go back to see what might have triggered his nose. While he was digging, I happened to get a closer look at that large log at the edge of our yard–you know, the one that Dad wants help with chopping up."

"Oh yeah, the one in the center of our property line by the small line of trees."

"Well, I found this lying on top of the log in between two branches. Luckily, Rupert was digging well below the fairy skeleton. I took Rupert back inside when I went to get an empty shoebox, and then I carried it carefully home to show you. Don't you think we should tell Mom and Dad now that we have evidence of fairies?"

"That would seem like a good idea." Evelyn paused, thinking of several scenarios that might occur if they told their parents. "Let's wait first; I just got a wonderful idea," she said, smiling broadly. "This might be just the thing we need to get on Ashkin's good side. I think we should first look up information on proper fairy burials, if there is such a thing. Wait, if we went ahead and buried the fairy skeleton ourselves, we might do something that is not a proper procedure in their realm. It might score us some points, though, if we take good care of the fairy body and offer it to Ashkin. It'd be a sort of goodwill offering. First, we need to find a place to store it, because I'm not keeping that box in my room."

"I don't really want to keep it in my room either," Reed retorted, mustering up a bit of bravery and trying not to appear fearful about sleeping in the same room with a dead fairy. "I'll just lock the box up in my closet until we figure out when to offer it to Ashkin. What happened at the fair judging?"

"Oh! I almost forgot to tell you. After I got my ribbon"– Evelyn paused, thinking back at the image–"I spotted a fairy flying right by Mom's head!"

Reed set the shoebox carefully on the highest shelf he could reach in his closet. "Do you think Mom spotted it?"

"No, I'm sure she didn't, but I saw the fairy give me a

thumbs-up after the cake judging. Hey, do you think they could have had anything to do with the cake winning the ribbon? I mean, the judge who tasted my cake couldn't put her finger on the flavors that she tasted." Her mind raced with possibilities. "Do you think that the fairies could have put something in my cake before I baked it?" The thought was disconcerting. She didn't want anyone to believe she was cheating to earn the purple ribbon, nor did she want the help. She wanted to earn the best ribbon all on her own; full credit can only be achieved with full effort. She thought back to when she'd made the cake and the unusual way it had deflated and then risen again. "Something else I'm wondering is, why did that fairy make herself known to me so clearly? There have been many weird things happening around here, and I'm confused—a lot of it has been downright mischievous, but a couple events have seemed positive."

"Hey, you're right. I've had so many wonderings about these fairies that I can't keep track." Reed picked up his science journal from his desk, now almost completely full.

As he flipped it open to the sections of fairy questions, Evelyn approached him, sharing the view of the notebook pages. "Is all of this on fairies?"

"Yeah. See, I've got my fairy observations in this first part, my fairy questions in the second part, my drawings and Internet pictures in the third part. Look! People have actually caught some of these fairies on camera."

Reed went to his tablet to pull up some of the websites he had viewed. He referred to his notebook for the correct address. "See, there they are."

Some of the online pictures looked authentic, but others were obviously fake.

"I know what you mean. Look at that one." Evelyn pointed to a picture of a man holding a large baby food jar with water in it, and on the bottom was a cutout picture of the famous Tinker Bell. "That looks like a picture cut from a storybook and put in a jar with liquid, which I'm assuming is formaldehyde like we used in science class, but the one on the other website looked just like the one I saw today."

"Ohhh, that just helped me think of another question," Reed said with delight. He quickly grabbed a pen and wrote something in his notebook. "Make that two questions that you helped me think of. *How long do fairies live? and How big do fairies get?*"

Evelyn started to leave. "I'd better get back to my room to put all my new school items away."

"You know, Evvie, I've decided that I really do like living in our new home. Every day seems like a new adventure."

"Remember, not a word about any of this fairy stuff to anyone at school, even if it's a couple of weeks away–not one soul!" Evelyn's voice was very stern. "You don't know how the other kids will treat the fairies. They'll probably want to get their paws on what we know and go to the pine woods, and you know we'd both be sick if there were a lot of other kids traipsing through the forest. The fairies would become angry, and who knows what they'd do! Oh, and I think that if Mom or Dad know about this stuff, they would scare the fairies away for good, or even more mischief might happen around the house!"

Reed thought Evelyn was too often right and that someday he wanted to be the one making more sensible points. They went down to dinner, and Evelyn shared her purple ribbon accomplishment with her father, who told them that the family would go together to the fair that weekend and view Evvie's ribbon on display.

* * *

Unable to sleep the next morning, Reed went straight to his computer to see if he could find answers to some of his questions. He had given up trying to capture a fairy in a trap a while ago, which allowed him to focus on more fact-finding.

Evelyn, still asleep in her room with her head between

pillows, was on the verge of waking up. A soft, repetitive tapping woke her, and she blinked slowly as she stretched her arms and legs. Once the sound of her rustling blankets subsided, she again heard the tapping. At first, she thought she could hear her heartbeat beneath the blankets.

"There it is again." She quickly looked at her window. Only a picture of a beautiful late-summer morning was evident through it, but a few minutes later, the tapping resumed. She thought a large dragonfly or some other insect was knocking at the window lightly, or maybe it was a woodpecker tapping. Getting out of bed and walking to the window, she fully opened the curtains. The tapping resumed yet again, and there she spotted the fairy she had seen the day before. At least she thought it was the same one. She stood watching the fairy flutter into view and out. The weather was beautiful, but very breezy.

Opening the window to see better, she caught the fairy struggling to fly against the strong wind gusts. She loosened the tabs to the window screen that ordinarily kept out insects. Once the screen was pushed out, the fairy saw her chance and swiftly flew into Evelyn's room. The fairy's movement was too fast for Evelyn to track. Her eyes scanned the ceiling, then her bed. She examined the floor, then behind the wastebasket. No view of the fairy. She shook out her blankets and finally moved some of the packages still on the floor from shopping the previous day.

"Where could that fairy be?" She opened her closet doors wider and looked all around when she heard a faint "Hello there!"

Evelyn quickly turned to her bed and then to her dresser. There she was! The faint glow of a bright golden light surrounded the fairy as if a protective aura enveloped her. She stood only about two inches high, but then seemed to grow another two inches within minutes. Evelyn didn't know if she was more perplexed, shocked, or curious, but she didn't feel threatened.

"Hello, Evelyn. I'm Natturia." The fairy's voice was soft and very high-pitched. "We will not hurt you—that is, unless you try to hurt us, but we've been watching you, and we think we understand where your heart lies." She quickly flew up and around Evelyn to get a better view of the human before her. With wings nearly as tall as she stood, Natturia had long silky hair that swept over her wings when they fluttered.

Evelyn was amazed at the shining golden color that reflected the light. "How do you know my name?"

"Oh, you and your family have been under our watch ever since you arrived in your home near the Grand Pines. That's what we call our forest home. You seem like kind humans, though Reed provided you with the location of our designated worship sector, and he tried to trap my brethren and me. He also captured a picture of our fairy life, and that was very worrisome to us. In fact, he took a photo of a momentous occasion in the life of a fairy." With her body seemingly so fragile and nearly translucent, Natturia walked around a small bottle of perfume that rested on the dresser and gave it a quick whiff. Turning back to address Evelyn, Natturia continued, "My father was very, very upset when he learned of the photograph that your brother took of us and that you and your family stepped foot on our sacred ground!"

"Well, I, uh, I mean . . . we *are* sorry. We had no idea. Who is your father, and why have you shown yourself to me?" Evelyn could hardly think straight, much less get her words out clearly.

"My father is Ashkin, and he is the leader of the Grand Pines tribe of fairies, although there are fairies higher ranking than my father. You seemed most helpful and respectful of nature. I watched you use the apples in your food creation with care and love. You've displayed respect toward nature, and you didn't waste the apples; even the parts you didn't use appeared to be going to another purpose and were not thrown away. We love to see no waste." Natturia smiled broadly.

"Oh, you mean those apple scraps. Yes, our mother

likes any food scraps to be put into the compost pile that she'll use for her garden." Evelyn watched the fairy investigate her dresser top while she spoke.

Soon, Evelyn heard a second, somewhat deeper, voice. "And you've cared for the plants in your home with love, food, and water." Evelyn looked for the source of the additional voice. "You are a thoughtful steward of nature, which is our home." The fairy with the deeper tone, a male, appeared from behind Evelyn's perfume bottle. "That is why our father sent us to talk to you. He wants to ensure that you are not an agent of the pixies and to enlist your help to fight those who have been much trouble for our clan. He also wants us to ask for your help in destroying the photo evidence of our family and friends."

"Wow, now I'm really confused." Evelyn's brain flooded with questions. She wanted to run and get Reed, but she knew that might scare the fairies away, so she decided to pose her questions one at a time and do all she could to be unthreatening. "Um, okay. Well, first of all, I've been introduced to Natturia. Who are you, and what's a pixie?" With the first question barely out of her mouth, Evelyn let out a giant, "Haaattchoooo!"

That small gust was enough to blow both fairies off the dresser almost to the floor, but they were able to regain their strength and change the momentum of the blast of air just before hitting the ground.

The male fairy sat up from where the two landed on the floor. "My name is Sampion. I am Natturia's brother and Ashkin's only son."

They darted back to the dresser top so fast that Evelyn had a very hard time tracking the fairies with her eyes as she grabbed a tissue.

"Oh, I'm so sorry. I didn't sneeze you off my dresser intentionally. I think some of that fairy dust from your wings made it to my nose. I hope my sneeze didn't hurt you."

Standing back atop Evelyn's dresser, Natturia and Sampion looked at each other, then to Evelyn. "If you mean us no harm, we understand, but if that is a ploy to harm us, then we shall work to make your life miserable," Sampion warned.

The two fairies straightened themselves up a bit. "Now where were we?" Sampion looked at Natturia and continued, "Pixies were once fairies long ago, but they trouble others with annoyances and mischief. They delight so much in creating trickery, and they are not helpful in our causes. They are also smaller in size than fairies, but collectively, they have much of our power. There was a time when we lived in the pine forest together harmoniously, but since the war, they have been cast out." Sampion sat on a trinket box on Evelyn's dresser.

Natturia pleaded, "Right now, we are here to enlist your help in the future of our home. The pixies cause us problems daily, and we are aware they have introduced a few for your family of humans as well. We need to make certain they won't do anything to help the humans take over our forest."

Sampion added, "Also, if other humans see the photograph of us in our habitat, they are sure to invade our homes to seek more information. We hate to think of the ruckus that will come if that photograph gets in the wrong hands." Sampion stood a bit taller than Natturia, though he was her younger brother, and he carried a long, sharp-edged javelin in his left hand. His very slender body stood strong, and his tiny, beady eyes stared forcefully, with his sharp jawline and chiseled forehead cutting a distinct angle from the top of his head toward his nose. Evelyn could see that Sampion was very serious as he spoke sternly. "We can share much information with you later, but you must first prove that you do, indeed, have an allegiance to our fairy tribe and that you will help save our home."

Evelyn's eyes were wide as she spoke, still surprised to see two fairies standing in front of her. "Sampion, Natturia, I'm still trying to take this all in. I met your father briefly, but I'm still new to the fairy community. I'll do anything I can to help you, but I think that it might be beneficial to enlist my brother's help as well. Besides, I have many so questions about fairies that need to be answered before I can really be of aid."

The breeze became so wickedly strong that Evelyn quickly turned her attention to the window. Outside the trees were blowing with great gusts, the tall grasses in the fields near their house bent close to the ground, and a large, dark cloud seemed to appear out of nowhere. Sheets of rain blew just outside her bedroom window.

"Oh no!" Natturia's voice filled with fear. "The pixies must know we're here. I'm sure of it! Why else would this storm appear out of nowhere?"

Evelyn could see the storm brewing right next to her window, but it didn't extend to other parts of the yard. She watched a completely dry car not using its windshield wipers drive by the house just beyond the yard, and the water fountain near the home's front entry had no visible rain dropping into it. Puzzled, Evelyn walked to close her window tightly and looked back toward the fairies.

"It's best we stay put for now until the rain and wind subside." Sampion looked at Evelyn.

Evelyn was shocked. "You mean pixies can change the weather?"

"Only in very small amounts," Natturia told her. "It might be a small quick rain shower, or a dust storm, or maybe a few streaks of lightning. Fairies can do the same, but we choose to do good with all of our powers. This storm is something the pixies would create." Natturia turned to focus on Evelyn. "The pixies must know Sampion and I are here talking to you, Evelyn. They know that fairies find it difficult to fly in strong winds and rain. We'll wait here until it passes."

Sampion continued, portraying a constant stance of warrior-like protector as he spoke proudly of his father, "Ashkin is the mightiest and wisest of all the fairies of these lands, and he helps to make sure that nature runs smoothly in this area. He and the Fairy Council rule the Grand Pine Woods with love and complete harmony."

Evelyn sat down again to take everything in. Natturia continued, "We love nature and all that it offers, and we have such respect for its beauty and complexities. Don't you think that nature often runs like a well-oiled machine? The bountiful raindrop, a long, slender blade of grass with its rough and smooth textures, and the delicious nectar the flowers offer us are some of the reasons we worship the land. We know Mother Nature doesn't always cooperate and that she can be destructive, but some of that can be blamed on human interference—or pixies. That is why we feel comfortable with you, Evelyn; you seem to love nature, too. We saw you pick up the trash bag that you found in our forest after your small human gathering with food in our home."

"You also show respect to even the smallest of creatures, like our spider friends," Sampion added. "It's that love you have that could help us conquer the pixies and remove them from our land, which is rightfully ours. Ashkin will see that you are well compensated for your troubles."

"I'd be happy to help you the best way that I can, but I think you are getting way ahead of yourselves, and I say that with all due respect, of course." Sweet-natured Evelyn was always the first to offer help where needed, but there was just too much she had to learn about fairies and pixies before she could even think of getting involved with either group, and she wanted Reed to join in. "Really, don't you think that two heads are better than one? I know Reed would love to help you too, and he does have a good heart. He's quite mature for his age, and he can be very compassionate." Evelyn felt that she was sort of selling the notion to the fairies, but she didn't want the responsibility of helping them to be just hers; she knew she was more effective working with Reed, and she knew he would be interested. Besides, she recalled her parents often telling her and Reed that 'Sticks in a bundle are unbreakable.'

A useful quote at this moment, she thought.

She quickly turned around when a knock at her bedroom door startled her.

"Are you up yet? We were beginning to think you weren't feeling well, Evelyn." Mrs. Gunderson, on a work-from-home day, opened the bedroom door. "You usually don't sleep this late. Everything okay?" She looked at Evelyn and then around the room.

"Um, oh, yes, Mom . . . I was just organizing one of my dresser drawers." Evelyn turned back to see if the fairies were still atop her dresser, then scanned the room to see where they may have flown to—up toward the ceiling, a glance near her desk, down by the wastebasket, and over near the closet doors—but there was no sign of them. "I'll be down to get breakfast as soon as I get changed."

"It won't be long before it's time for lunch. Oh, and I forgot to tell you that I picked up the pictures you and Reed took, and I set the envelope on your desk. Maybe later you two can share your photos with us." As she turned to leave, she announced, "Also, we're going to the fair this afternoon since it's the best fit for Dad's schedule." She looked out Evelyn's window to see the rain. Very puzzled, she uttered, "Hmm, that's odd. It was perfectly sunny in the back of the house. I might have to talk to your dad about alternative plans . . ." Mrs. Gunderson's voice trailed off as she left the room.

Evelyn quickly got dressed while scanning the room frantically for the fairies. She had no idea whether or not she should divulge the encounter to Reed, and now the photos were in her possession. Once her mom left, she immediately opened the envelope to view the pictures, thumbing through photos of cakes and the forest. She stopped at the photo Reed had taken at the tail end of the fairy's birth ritual, and it was clear why Natturia and Sampion wanted to keep it away from the wrong hands. The bottom of the tree was primarily centered in the photo, with two ants about to exit the scene through a small opening of the tree's base. Higher up, in the background, was the sight of two fairies blessing the area and the newborn. Indeed, this was the photograph that the fairies wanted destroyed, but Evelyn knew Reed would be expecting to see it. What was the best course of action? Perhaps the fairies were still in her room and could guide her.

"Natturia. Sampion. Where are you?" She continued to look in her closet, under the bed, in her trinket box. They were nowhere to be found, and she was taking too much time to get downstairs to breakfast. Deciding to keep mum about her encounter with the fairies and the pictures until she had more information, she hid the photos on her chest of drawers beneath a stack of clothes and proceeded downstairs, where she found Reed helping their mother clean dishes.

"Look, Evvie, I'm helping Mom with breakfast *and* the dishes. You owe me one because Dad said we can go to the fair as soon as we clean up the kitchen."

Mrs. Gunderson looked over the dish she was drying and could see that Evelyn was empty-handed. "Evelyn, aren't you going to share the photos with your brother?"

"Oh, I forgot to bring them down with me."

"Oh! Fantastic! You picked up the photos from the store, Mom? I can't wait to see how they turned out!"

"I'll show them to you later. Do you remember all the pictures we took of my baking? I'd like to sort through those first." Getting all too skilled at thinking up excuses, Evelyn found a way to buy time before Reed had his hands on the photographs. Maybe she could redirect his attention some more. "All right, Reed, what is your rush to go to the fair? I don't want to go when it's"–Evelyn looked at the bright sunshine outside their glass patio doors–"raining. What is happening with the weather? Did you listen to the forecast?"

"Yes," Reed announced, "and there was no mention of rain for today. Just look at that beautiful weather outside. Dry, sunny, very comfortable temps. What more could you ask for?"

Closing the cupboard after the dishes were put away, Mrs. Gunderson suggested, "We'd better listen to see if there are any weather changes, Reed. I just came down from Evelyn's room a few minutes ago, and I could see it storming outside her window."

Evelyn watched Reed dash upstairs to see what their mom was referring to, as he surely didn't want the threat of rain to ruin their plans. Fortunately for Evelyn, Reed's fair excitement temporarily erased his desire to look for the pictures as he ran back and reported to his mother.

"What rain? It's sunny out Evelyn's room, too," he announced.

Mrs. Gunderson looked surprised that a passing storm could disappear that suddenly, and she peered out the patio window in the kitchen, wondering where the clouds might have gone. But there was no sign of inclement weather—only clear skies filled with warm sunshine brightening the day. "Looks like we can go after all!"

"I'll go upstairs to get ready. I'll be quick about it." Evelyn rushed to her room, still eating some of her breakfast bar, with Reed close behind.

"Hey, Evelyn. Can I have a look at those pictures?"

"Yeah, sure," Evelyn said. "But make it quick. We don't have much time before we get going." *Drat!* she thought to herself. *I hoped he wouldn't think to bring those up!*

Reed opened the envelope with all the photographs and pulled out the fairy picture to examine it more closely. "What a great day! We get to go to the fair, and I have absolute proof with my photo of the fairies!" He beamed. "Yep, this is it. My proof!"

Evelyn's stomach turned a little. How was she going to get that picture back? She knew she would have to convince Reed that the picture should be destroyed as soon as possible.

While she finished putting her hair in a ponytail, she suggested, "We should really keep all the pictures together for now. Mom and Dad want to get going to the fair."

"Oh, all right." He slid the fairy photo back in the envelope. "Don't forget that I want that photo when we get back."

* * *

It was a picture-perfect day to attend the fair. After a first stop for food—a fair staple of hot dogs that were quickly gobbled down—the family quickly found the area where Evelyn's cake was displayed. In fact, many other fairgoers had found her entry, and there was a rather large crowd gathered in front of the display case. The kids exchanged puzzled glances.

"What's everyone looking at?" Reed asked as he moved ahead into a small open space.

He sneaked up to the front of the display where he could get a close view, but only after Evelyn inquired, "Why do you suppose everyone is standing in front of my cake?"

Evelyn nervously looked at her parents for an answer. She walked toward the crowd, but there was barely any room for her to squeeze in, and most people were much taller than she was. Her parents walked behind her and managed to get a better look once the others moved aside. Finally, Evelyn was close enough to see her fair entry. There it was in plain view–the dessert sat on a pretty silver cake tier with the slice the judge tasted earlier removed, and to Evelyn, it was as plain as day. A shadowy silhouette closely resembling a fairy lay within the dessert amid the apple pieces. But most who saw her dessert wouldn't notice the fairy, who seemed to be part of the layers of stacked baked apples. Questions about how and when it got there entered into Evelyn and Reed's heads. Poor Evelyn. There wasn't a thing she could do about it.

Midwest Country Apple Pastry Cake

Pastry Crust

1½ cups	flour
½ teaspoon	kosher salt
8 tablespoons	unsalted butter, cold and cut into small pieces
5–6 tablespoons	ice water
	cooking spray or butter

Place flour, salt, and chilled butter in the bowl of a food processor. Mix until butter has been cut into small pieces throughout flour/salt mixture.

While pulsing processor, add cold water slowly until pastry mixture holds together. Turn dough out onto plastic film and wrap. Chill in fridge for 2+ hours. Roll dough onto floured surface and roll out pastry to use as crust. Spray 10-inch springform pan with cooking spray or brush sides and bottom of pan with melted butter. Place crust inside prepared springform pan. Preheat oven to 400 degrees. Place springform pan on cookie sheet lined with parchment paper.

Apple Filling

12–13	large apples, peeled, cored, and sliced about ⅛-inch thick
1½ tablespoons	lemon juice (fresh)
⅓ cup	currants, plumped in hot water and drained
1 cup	golden raisins
1½ tablespoons	cornstarch

⅓	cup brown sugar
1¼ tablespoons	cinnamon
¼ tablespoon	cardamom, ground
¼ tablespoon	nutmeg, ground

Mix apples and lemon juice with plumped currants and raisins. Toss with spices. Pour into prepared crust. Place top layer of apples in a symmetrical pattern for an attractive presentation. There should be enough apples to reach the top of the springform pan. Cover lightly while baking with tinfoil if top of pasty cake is too brown. Bake 60-75 minutes. Using a fork, check apples for desired tenderness. Bake 10-15 minutes for more tender apples. While apples bake, prepare vanilla sauce below.

Vanilla Sauce

9 tablespoons	butter, melted
1 cup	brown sugar
½ cups	cream
2 tablespoons	bourbon (alcohol will bake off, but may substitute vanilla)
2 tablespoons	cornstarch
2 teaspoons	cinnamon
5	eggs
	powdered sugar
	or 2–3 tablespoons apple jelly, melted

In a bowl, mix melted butter, sugar, cream, flavoring, cornstarch, cinnamon, and eggs. Pour over apple cake, making sure sauce evenly covers apples and falls in between layers as much as possible. Bake for another 20 minutes. Cool on wire rack. Dust with powdered sugar or brush with melted apple jelly.

7.

The Pine Encounter

Finding a fairy in the cake was a heartache for Evelyn and Reed. They tried their best to concentrate on the sights and sounds of the fair after, but they dreaded hearing what their parents were going to say about the cake.

"Your purple ribbon got a lot of people's attention, Evelyn! I'm very, very proud of you," Mr. Gunderson said, beaming.

"Thanks, Dad. I'm very proud of myself, too. I had no idea my dessert would be so well received, but I did work long and hard at trying to find the best apple flavor, and people have always raved about Grandma's recipe." Evelyn gave Reed a curious glance. Why hadn't their dad mentioned anything about the fairy in the pie cake? Did her parents not see it? She wanted desperately to talk to Reed about it, without their parents listening in.

At last, a chance looked available when the elder Gundersons said they wanted to check out the tent with the art exhibits.

"That's all right, Mom and Dad. You go ahead without us. Reed and I will take a break and just sit and chat as soon as we find a bench. We'll wait here for you to come out of the art building. Take your time," said Evelyn.

The parents disappeared into the art exhibit building, and Evelyn and Reed grabbed the opportunity to have a private discussion.

"Evelyn! What, exactly, was that in your cake?" Reed asked accusingly. "It looked like you baked an entire fairy into it! I'm sure you didn't do that on purpose, but why didn't you tell me that you caught an actual fairy?"

"Reed! I didn't catch a fairy, and I certainly didn't put one in my dessert! It must have fallen in when I stirred the batter, or maybe it simply attached itself to the cake after the judge removed a slice." Evelyn tried to recall sitting adjacent to the Mrs. Winston only the day before. She paused, looking down as if she'd find the answer somewhere on the floor. "I don't remember seeing the fairy in or on the cake when the judge cut into it. Nope, I distinctly recall watching the judge cut my dessert, and there was no evidence of a fairy anywhere on that cake. The only fairy I saw that day was the one that gave me a thumbs-up after the judging. Also, the one in my cake looks like a male fairy anyway, and the one I saw was female. What do you suppose Mom and Dad think about my cake? Neither of them said anything about the fairy."

"I think Dad was focused on the ribbon you earned *next* to the cake. Besides, he's seen your cakes so many times before. Maybe he just didn't look at it in too much detail. Otherwise, I'm sure he would've said something . . . but I wonder if that's what the crowd was looking at."

"Maybe you're right. I know Mom already saw my cake at judging, and she didn't say anything about a fairy, so we probably don't have much to worry about, and I'll just have to let people think what they will about my cake. Who knows? Maybe they were discussing the ribbon I received."

Evelyn desperately wanted to tell Reed about meeting Natturia and Sampion, but she didn't want to risk upsetting the fairies, and now she'd have to tell them about what was found on–or in–her cake. She decided to bring the focus back to the fairy that Reed and Rupert had found in the backyard. "We'd better talk more about the shoebox with the fairy's body."

"Oh yeah, we've absolutely got to get that back to the pine woods! I'll bet the fairies would appreciate that we returned the deceased to them. Don't you think?" He didn't mention anything more about the topic, afraid that being uncomfortable sleeping with a fairy corpse in his closet would be information Evelyn could use against him at a later date.

"Yeah, we'd better get that taken care of just as soon as we get back home!"

* * *

The Gunderson family soon returned home after their busy afternoon at the fair.

"We'll be up in our rooms, Mom," Evelyn called as she ascended the stairs. "I might even take a little rest." Evelyn knew very well that her head was wandering far too much to settle down enough and catch any true rest.

She followed Reed to his room as he carefully reached into his closet for the shoebox, checked inside, and, satisfied with the contents, announced, "Let's go to the forest now, Evelyn."

"All right, but I have an idea. Why don't we try entering the woods from another side this time?" Evelyn would have to offer a convincing reason if she really wanted to help the fairies.

"Why would we do that?"

Evelyn could only think of what Natturia and Sampion had said to her about the family picnicking on their sacred area, and she didn't want to repeat that mistake by treading over the same area again. She wanted to be respectful of the fairy protocol for burial. Besides, she also had to keep in mind that Sampion and Natturia were possibly still in her bedroom.

"It'll only take a few more minutes to walk to the other side of the pines; I've wanted to check out that area for some time. You never know if there's something interesting to discover, and I'd like to check out the lone oak tree on the other side of the pine forest. Let's get going, and carry that shoebox very carefully."

Rupert began to sniff and scratch at something under the closet door.

"What are you doing, Rupert?" Worried Rupert had caught Natturia's or Sampion's scent, Evelyn opened the closet door and was relieved to find only a small black spider crawling under one of her shoes. "Grab a tissue, quickly, Reed."

Reed casually but gently cupped his hands around the spider. "It seems like there are bugs everywhere I turn in this new house."

"Fine. Let's get going."

Evelyn grabbed the spider gently with a tissue with Rupert following closely behind. "Nope, sorry, pal," she commanded the dog. "You have to stay behind. We'll be right back." She knew he would not be welcome in the pine woods and would be rather disruptive when they returned the fairy's body. She also felt a strong desire to focus on what was taking place and didn't want to divert her attention in any way.

They left their house while their parents were conveniently preoccupied, and this time, they walked around to the right side of the pine grove all the way to the back, where a giant oak tree loomed over the pines. With its wide girth, the very knotted oak tree looked solidly strong with years of weathering. Evelyn wondered what stories it would tell about the comings and goings of small forest creatures if it had a voice. The branches were spaced far enough apart that Reed could tackle climbing it easily, but for now, they needed to find a good entry point into the woods.

"Over here," whispered a small voice. Evelyn looked at Reed to see if he, too, had heard the faint call, but he kept walking with the shoebox gripped firmly in hand.

"Evelyn, enter the pine woods east of the tree. Don't go beyond that point," Sampion directed as he and Natturia fluttered nearby.

Evelyn directed Reed to the edge of the pines, saying, "Let's go in this way, Reed."

"Oh, all right." He really wanted to be the one who decided where to bury the fairy, but after a hectic day, he, too, was feeling tired and decided to let Evelyn put her energy into locating a burial site.

They entered the forest, where they ducked around lower branches, stepping over a smaller growth of plants. Hovering in the air before them were Natturia and Sampion.

"Why, hello, Natturia and Sampion." Evelyn bowed her head to the fairies in respect.

"How do you know their names?" Reed asked, suddenly becoming reenergized. "Natturia? Sampion? What kind of names are those?" He sounded a bit impudent, which was odd because he was really not the disrespectful type, but his energy was depleted, and he felt he had done so much research on the subject of fairies already, he should have been the one that the fairies befriended first. *He* had been the one with the most interest and enthusiasm in the entire world of fairies, not Evelyn.

"I met these fairies by accident just this morning. I didn't say anything to you because we were busy all day, and I had no idea how they'd react if I told you."

"What? You didn't tell me that you met *actual* fairies?"

Reed was indignant, but Sampion quickly assured him that it was not Evelyn's decision.

"We initially had no intention of telling you, Reed, about our identity," Sampion continued. "This rite of passage is too important not to reveal ourselves, and Evelyn has earned our utmost respect and trust at this point."

"Because you are her brother and we saw how respectful you were with our spider friend earlier, we are trusting you, as well, to keep our identities secret and to be loving to our home, the Grand Pine Woods," added Natturia.

"Yes, ma'am." Reed was so excited to be actually talking to real fairies that he almost forgot he was carrying important cargo. "Oh, boy, have I got a lot of questions for you guys!"

"We do not have time now for questions, Reed," Sampion warned. "We are here to bury our dead. There will be plenty of time to answer your questions later. Right now, if you want to maintain our respect for you, you will honor us by helping to bury one of our own."

Remembering why they'd made the trek to the woods, Reed whispered to Evelyn, "How do they already know why we're here?"

Natturia directed her response to Reed. "We heard your plans when we were in Evelyn's room earlier. We rushed back to the woods to notify our elders of your plans prior to your arrival."

"Of course. What would you like us to do first?" Reed was only too happy to help.

"You will need to measure the length of the corpse with your hands. That is how deep to dig a hole, and the hole only needs to be wide enough for the corpse to fit vertically–feet first."

"You don't need it to lie down?" Evelyn inquired.

"No, even the dead must be in an alert position, as they always must be when alive," Natturia explained. "One never knows if the Fairy Council will need those fairies to help in future battles, and if it is decided that they are needed, they will have new life breathed into them, especially if the task or opponent seems too big to overcome with our current infantry."

Just then, Evelyn and Reed could see hundreds of fireflies lined up row upon row right outside the forest.

Reed looked around at the site. "What's happening?"

The fear in his voice trailed as Natturia answered calmly and matter-of-factly, "Those are lightning bugs who have come to pay their respects to our family of fairies. We consider them extended family just as we do with all of nature's living things, Reed, and we show them kindness and love. We do not trap them."

Reed wasn't sure if she was referring to the trap he'd

set for the fairies in the tree or the traps he'd made for lightning bugs in the past. "Um, I'll take down that trap I set soon, Natturia, and I won't trap anymore lightning bugs in jars. Promise." He was a bit embarrassed, as he was typically a rule follower and a compassionate young man.

Natturia only smiled.

"Now let's get this ceremony completed." Sampion pointed to a large stick to use for digging.

Because the corpse was so small, the digging process took little time, though the children wanted to make sure the hole was an adequate depth.

Natturia quickly added, "We'll finish the rest." With that, she blew a small amount of sparkly dust into the burial hole, making it smooth and even around the edges.

Reed didn't hesitate to ask, "If you could do that, then why didn't you create the entire hole for burial?"

"Reed, you are still young and inquisitive. We will assume you are questioning us because of your age and not because you are to any degree disrespectful," Sampion flashed back.

"Oh, no, sir." Reed wasn't completely certain even how to correctly address these fairies–Your Honor, as he had addressed Ashkin? Or perhaps Your Majesty? Ma'am? Sir?

"Reed, we are observing very closely your degree of loyalty to the fairies," Sampion said.

Evelyn slowly removed the fairy's body from the shoe-box and placed it upright into the narrow hole. She turned to the hovering fairies who were overseeing the whole process, then Sampion blew a very small amount of iridescent dust, causing the burial hole to seal and disappear completely to the naked eye.

"Where did the burial hole go? Don't you put a grave marker or headstone on it so that you can pay your respects later?" Reed had so many questions.

Natturia understood his curiosity. "If we pointed out our beloved dead and their burial plots to our enemies, we would give our enemies ammunition to use against us later, and when you are this small, enemies are plentiful."

They all bowed their heads in prayer and then began to return home. Before the children could take even two steps, Evelyn was compelled to say, "Excuse me, but there is another matter we have to ask you about before we go."

Natturia and Sampion turned around. Reed noticed the fluorescent aura that surrounded each of them subsided while they listened. When they were moving, the aura glowed brightly, and when they became less active, their auras dimmed.

"There is something we must discuss with you right away, and we really have no idea how it happened or what to do about it." Evelyn recounted the spectacle at the county fair from the moment she'd made the apple dessert to their discovery of the fairy earlier in the day. She knew there was no reason to feel guilty, but she couldn't help noticing the feeling seep into her mind just a little. "I honestly have no idea how a fairy got into the cake; at least it wasn't there when we first sliced into it."

Natturia and Sampion looked at each other in agreement. "That was likely the act of a pixie," Sampion suggested.

"Or it might have been a simple accident, Sampion." Evelyn usually gave people–even pixies–the benefit of the doubt.

"You don't think the pixies are capable of interfering with the simple task of baking a cake?" Sampion turned to Evelyn. "Had there been any strange events in your home before you made the cake? Any acts around your dwelling for which you have no explanation?"

Evelyn and Reed stood staring at each other for the longest time. Racing through their memories were images of unexplained events in their new house: the broken cup, Reed's disappearing space glider, Evelyn's cakes, the floating egg. The list was growing.

"It *is* the pixies!" they said almost in unison.

"We've been knocking our heads, wondering what was going on. We thought maybe Ashkin was behind it, but that was before we knew fairies use their powers for good," Evelyn continued.

"Ashkin may have given you a warning, but he would not have played such pranks. You must know that pixies are more powerful when working together. Those actions you have listed seem to be individual mischievous tricks on their part. Wait until they join together and decide to work as one. Then you will not have any doubt as to who is behind these actions."

"Ewwwwwwwww, do you think I baked the fairy? Just how did it get on or in my cake?" Evelyn was horrified at the thought.

"It is possible, Evelyn. It is also quite possible that the pixies put a fairy that they had captured into your cake after it was baked," explained Natturia.

"I'm getting confused." Evelyn paused in thought. "I was sure I saw a fairy give me a thumbs-up after the judging, but now I wonder if it was pixie I saw instead. Maybe the pixies were glad I did their dirty work for them by baking a fairy." The color drained from her face as she thought back to seeing the image in her cake. If she unknowingly assisted the pixies—well, she could barely stand the thought. She couldn't decide if she was more horrified or more angry at the moment.

Sampion responded, "We don't want you to feel

distressed, Evelyn. And, Reed, I will relay to you what Natturia and I have already asked of your sister since I now believe that you, too, will respect the lives of fairies. You see, pixies are very much like fairies. However, their actions can be considered anything from playfully annoying to harmful or injurious. I suppose they were testing you in your home to see how you'd cope and where your future allegiances would lie. Now that you have chosen to be our allies, beware of future pixie actions."

"Thank you, Sampion. We'll definitely be on our guard. I'd like to think that Reed and I can be friends with both fairies and pixies, but right now, all I can feel is anger if they messed with my cake and the fairies. Whether that was their idea of a laugh or not, I can see why fairies have to be defensive."

Reed interjected, "We appreciate your warning and hope that we can count on your help if we need it in the future, just as you can count on our help if we're able to do something for you."

"If your allegiances to us remain strong and consistent, then all you have to do to summon us is close your eyes. Then clear your mind, wholly concentrate on us, and clear your heart of evil. Still your body and summon us. We will feel your energy," Natturia instructed.

"Good to know!" Evelyn felt securer with those

directions, and she'd make sure that Reed followed those instructions when needed.

"Will we see pixies in action?" Reed looked around to see if there might be a chance of catching a pixie in the area.

"You should not expect to see a pixie in our pine forest home, but you may see a pixie when you least expect it elsewhere." Natturia continued, "While fairies love nature and enjoy the help we give to nature, pixies can seldom be trusted even though they may appear friendly. Typically, if trouble arrives, it's a pixie who is behind it in some fashion."

"Yeah, sure. It would've been easy to think that someone in our family lost the keys or changed the clocks, but not when you look at all the things that have happened."

Evelyn nodded as she focused on the fairies before them. "I understand what you mean, Reed."

Natturia added, "They are fickle and often cause hurt, especially for those who appear to be good. You will learn much more as time goes by. Just be on your toes, and know that pixies have a particular fondness for ribbons and horses. And, Reed, we know that you captured the image of fairies with your camera. You must destroy that immediately."

Sampion said, "Do not allow that the picture to land in the wrong hands. It will surely result in opening a Pandora's box of trouble."

With that, the fairies flew off, and the children walked quickly home, as it wouldn't be long before dark.

"Don't you see, Reed, that we have to destroy the picture you took of the fairies? I don't think you want to be responsible if that picture gets into the wrong hands, and we want to help the fairies any way possible."

Reed remained silent and kept walking, too tired to hold a conversation but also too busy recollecting everything the fairies had told him.

Mrs. Gunderson, hyper-focused while working at the family computer, looked toward the patio door as the kids entered. "Where have you two been? I thought you were tired after the busy afternoon at the fair."

"Oh, um, well, we were just on a walk by the pine forest," Reed stammered a little.

Suddenly interested, Mrs. Gunderson added, "What's so fascinating in the pine forest? It's not like it changes much over time."

Evelyn replied, "Well, we wanted to check out that big oak tree behind the pines. We hadn't been there yet. Do we have any ribbon, Mom?"

"What kind? We've got wrapping ribbon, and we've got material ribbon. Take your pick. They're both in the craft room." She returned her attention to the computer. "Are you two headed to your rooms? There's fruit in the fridge if you're hungry."

"Thanks, Mom. I'll get ready for bed and then come down for a banana," announced Evelyn. Before she went to her room, she rummaged through the craft basket, where she found and cut two large pieces of ribbon for herself and Reed.

Upstairs, she found Reed playing the usual game of tug-of-war in his room with Rupert. "Here, Reed, which ribbon do you want to have?"

"What do I need ribbon for?"

"You heard what the fairies told us; pixies are attracted to horses and ribbons, and we want to be able to get on the good side of the pixies. Maybe then they'll stop messing with us in our new home."

"Great. I've got a ribbon to attract pixies. Are you going to give me a carrot for horses, too?" Reed chuckled.

"Of course not, but we might be able to walk to that horse farm down the road. It wouldn't hurt to just look around."

"I don't want to walk three miles to the horse farm, Evvie, but then again, I don't feel like doing much of anything right now." Reed fell on his bed with his face flat on the pillow.

"I know. All I feel like doing now is reading a little and then hitting the hay, but I was just thinking that we brought up the idea of visiting that horse farm before with Mom and Dad. They give riding lessons there, you know."

"Oh yeah. I remember."

"It wouldn't hurt anything to go for a look, and Mom and Dad would just think we're there to see the horses—which I *would* be because I love horses, anyways. We would simply have two keen sets of eyes also scoping out any sign of a pixie." Her eyebrows rose the way they did whenever she had a great idea. "And you can tuck your ribbon safely in your pocket. I'll wear mine in my hair. When we visit the horse farm, we might be more likely to see the pixies if we each have a ribbon."

"I suppose that'd work. I do wonder . . . don't you think that pixies are just a naughty version of a fairy?"

"I imagine that's how you can describe them."

Reed's mind wandered. "Maybe they're troublemakers because they aren't as tall or as beautiful as fairies. You know, like how so many people seem to compare themselves to others." His mind swam with all sorts of fairy wonderings, and he forgot all about the picture of the fairies for now. "Do you want to find a pixie so we can see what they look like?"

"I'm not sure at this point. Part of me would be too scared to interact with a pixie because I don't know much about them, and I'm still mad at that cake stunt they pulled. Right now, all I want to do is get to sleep. It's been a long day, and I'm super tired."

"Do you think we'll see one of the fairies again soon?" Reed paused for moment. "I wonder where they sleep at night."

"Good night, Reed. Save your questions for tomorrow, and write down your observations in your notebook." Evelyn turned to retreat to her room for the night after turning off the bedroom ceiling lights, leaving the soft, warm glow of the lamp on the nightstand.

"Great idea, Evelyn! Good night."

Reed wasted no time in locating his notebook, and he busily jotted down his thoughts and illustrations from the busy day while they were fresh on his mind.

Mrs. Gunderson stopped by Reed's room, followed by her husband.

"It's getting really late, Reed. I thought you'd be fast asleep by now," she said.

"Good night, Reed. I'll let Rupert outside. You'd better finish getting ready for bed," Mr. Gunderson reminded Reed before calling, "Come on, Rupert! Better get outside before Reed shuts off all the lights."

"Oh, all right. Dad, do you think we can go visit that horse farm a couple of miles north tomorrow?"

"Sure, I don't see why not. We'll have time after church, but we'll just go to check out the facility. We can find out more about what this farm offers when we're there. We won't ride any of the horses just yet. Right now, I think we all need a good night's sleep."

Evelyn was in her room, still awake enough to remember to go retrieve the photo of the fairies. She thought to tuck it under her mattress until she found the perfect time to destroy it. She was far too tired to think more.

* * *

Before church, Reed rushed to Evelyn's room to inquire about the fairy photo. "Where's the picture of the fairies? I wanted to put it in my science journal."

Evelyn looked in the mirror to finish putting on a necklace. "Did you forget that Natturia and Sampion specifically asked us to destroy that photo?"

"I remember. I just didn't see any harm if I glued it to one of my pages in my notebook."

"Then you must've forgotten what the fairies said could happen if we *don't* destroy it." If Reed kept the picture, he might lose it, the wrong set of eyes might see it, or other circumstances could play out, and she didn't want to take any chances. "If the fairies found out that we didn't destroy the picture like they asked, who knows what they could do to us?"

"Yeah, maybe you're right." Reed returned to his room, disappointed but determined to put the picture in his science notebook regardless. Keeping the picture might come in handy in the future. Who knew? Maybe he would get a favor from the fairies in exchange for the picture.

Reed planned to retrieve the photo when Evelyn brushed her teeth; however, when he riffled through the pictures, it was gone! "Evelyn! Where's that picture? I want to see it again before we get rid of it."

"Hey, get out of my room! I told you that I put it in a safe place until we can figure out the best way to destroy it."

Reed seethed. He hated that Evelyn controlled the picture he'd taken, and he set his mind on finding it. "What gives her the right to hide that picture? I'm the one who took it after all, so it belongs to me! I *will* find that picture!" Reed told himself as he turned to go to his room.

"We've got to get going, Reed. Mom and Dad are calling us down for church."

Reed told himself that he might return to retrieve the picture later, without Evelyn's knowledge, but maybe he could find the opportunity now. "I'll be right down. I need to change my shirt first," he called. "I spilled some food on it at breakfast."

As Evelyn left, Reed quickly changed shirts and ran to Evelyn's room. *Now where would Evelyn put that picture for safekeeping? It shouldn't be too hard to find. I know all her secret hiding places.*

He only had a couple of minutes to look. The jewelry box and her desk drawer yielded nothing. Then he remembered one of Evelyn's favorite hiding spots. Feeling under her mattress, he slid his hands down the length of it until . . . success!

Running to his room, he stuck the photo in his notebook until he could find the best place to glue it later. For now, he quickly straightened Evelyn's bedsheets and dashed downstairs to join the family.

"What took you so long, Reed? We're going to be late for church if we don't hurry," Dad said.

* * *

Gunderson family church time, a meal out, and then a quick car ride to the River's Edge Horse Farm Training Facility followed. They had passed the horse training facility several times daily on their way to home from the city limits. There were two other horse farms in the area, but this one was closest to their house and situated between the river and the county road. The grazing pastures were sep-arated into four large pens used by about twenty Arabian horses at different times of the week, with a large feeding trough that several horses stood around if they weren't grazing in the pastures. At the end of the long driveway sat a large barn with its door partly open, housing the hay bales, followed by the owner's house and then the horse training facility. Evelyn and Reed didn't know if they were more excited at seeing the horses up close or pos-sibly catching a glimpse of a pixie in its preferred habitat.

The family's muffled conversation stopped abruptly as they entered the dark building. Dust particles floated through the air as light poured through the open door.

"Reed, doesn't this smell just like the stables we walked through when we visited the horse barns at the state fair?" Evelyn looked toward the staging area for the horses. "Look, this must be where they tie a horse to prep it be-fore the show."

The family entered quietly so as not to startle the horses. A tall, lean young lady with knee-high boots and a riding helmet pulled a chestnut-colored horse behind her. The horse, with white markings on its legs that reminded Reed of long stockings, walked with a steady *clip-clop, clip-clop, clip-clop, clip-clop.*

"Evelyn, can you reach high enough to look into this

stall?" Her dad pointed to one of the horses that stood nibbling on the bits of hay beneath him behind a fastened chest-high gate.

"This horse is named Pennies from Heaven," pointed out one of the staff members as she grabbed the horse's bit and halter, "and that horse there is named Lolita." To the left of the horse stalls was a large area where spectators watched one of the horses exercise on a lead.

"I wonder if that horse gets dizzy going in circles around and around and around," said Reed, chuckling.

Evelyn ignored him, instead focused on the many new sites and keeping an eye out for pixies. She whispered to Reed, "I just wish we could ask the horses themselves or the staff if they've ever seen a pixie in this area."

"I'm sure they'd just tell you that they have to shoo anything that flies and they don't really pay attention to see if it's an insect or a pixie."

Evelyn glanced back at Reed with the same parental look that meant remarks like that were wholly unappreciated. She turned to her mom. "Do you think we can come back sometime for a riding lesson or a group ride on the horses?"

"Kids, I think that sounds like a fantastic idea and a lot of fun, but we'd better see how busy your school schedules look first. The temperatures outside will be getting a little cooler, and it won't be long before it's fall. Dad and I'll check out what sorts of horse rides this place offers, and we'll look at our schedules, too." Turning to Reed, Mrs. Gunderson asked, "What do you think? Would you like to come back and go horseback riding sometime?"

Without hesitation, Reed said, "I'd love to! I saw some information on a table when we came in. If you stay here, I can go back and grab some of it."

Not waiting for an answer, he briskly walked back to the entrance. On his left was a brown horse with white and dark brown patches, and behind it, Reed caught a glimpse of what he thought was a hefty, oversized horse-fly. He brushed it away as it buzzed and buzzed around his head.

***

Returning home in the car later, Evelyn thought of how to get back to the horse farm again without too much time passing so they could, indeed, have a successful pixie sighting. They drove cautiously through the beautiful countryside down the road adjacent to their home, as deer crossed unexpectedly out of the tall cornfields. Evelyn noticed three geese in the distance fly in the same direction as the car, but as she looked more closely at them, she could see that they were not geese at all. Instead, hovering just a few feet above the car, was something else entirely.

Were these dragonflies speeding in the air near their car? She did not lose sight of them until their car entered the garage. She looked out the back window to quickly catch the direction and, perhaps, a closer look at these winged aliens.

"Evelyn, what are you doing?"

"Oh, I thought I saw some geese flying in the distance, or least it looked like geese, and I was just following where they might be headed. Thanks, Mom and Dad, for taking us to the horse farm. I had a good time. Didn't you, too, Reed?"

As they waited for a reply, Evelyn saw an empty space where Reed had been seated in the car. He hadn't wasted a moment leaving, and by the time Evelyn was done gazing at the objects, he had already returned to his bedroom to locate his science journal. He found just the spot where he hoped to affix the fairy photograph, and quickly glued it in.

Putting the literature about the horse facility on the kitchen counter, Evelyn then joined Reed in his room. "What are you jotting down?"

Reed felt relieved that he'd remembered to take care of the photo before Evelyn returned. "Didn't you see them? I don't know if they were pixies or fairies, but I don't want to forget those bugs or whatever they were. I've got to write down as many observations as I can think of while they're fresh in my mind."

"Gosh, I wasn't sure if we would see any pixies on our first trip to the horse farm, and I'm not sure what I saw outside the car window. What did you see?"

"I saw those insects or creatures flying fast–so fast that I don't even know what they were. They were darker in color than the fairies, and they had large wings for their body size, and"–Reed looked around to make sure there would be no additional ears listening–"I actually wondered if what we saw might be actual pixies, because I swatted one of those creatures kinda hard when we were in that horse training facility. I didn't intend to hurt it; it's just that it was incredibly annoying. It kept buzzing around my ears and face while I went to get the brochures. When I couldn't take it anymore, I just had enough and flung my arm out as it was making a lunge at my head. That's when it happened."

He carefully pulled out the ribbon from his pocket, which was wrapped around a small bundle. "Honestly, it was just an accident. I thought at first that I hit one of those large horseflies, but when I looked down, I could see that I'd hit something else. I didn't know what it was, so I just wrapped it in the ribbon to get a better look at it when we got back home. You were watching the horses in the arena, so I put it in my pocket until we could check it out later. I'd bet that what you and I saw flying next to the car were some pixies coming after me for swatting one of their own." He looked worried as he glanced up to Evelyn and set the bundled ribbon on his desk. He pulled the ribbon gently to reveal a fragile and crumpled dark mass. Evelyn and Reed bent down to closely examine it and, without saying a word, Reed took a pencil to gently unfold a crumpled wing from the body and then lift the other wing. It was apparent that whatever he'd hit was regaining its senses, so he looked around his room for something to contain it. In his closet was a jar he'd often used to catch lightening bugs.

"What are you doing?" Evelyn stopped him from trapping the entity on his desk. "We promised the fairies that we wouldn't try to trap them anymore."

"Look closely, Evelyn! Does this look like any of the fairies we've seen? I'm not planning on keeping it; I just want to get a better look at it, figure out what it is, and when it's in better shape, I'll maybe return it outside. I can't really be blamed for trying to catch what I think is an oversized annoying bug."

Under the glass jar, the small entity began to unravel more–very slowly at first. With the wind apparently knocked out of it, the being slowly moaned in a tiny voice and stretched as it regained its consciousness and strength. Before much time passed, it stood under the mason jar before Evelyn and Reed, who stood frozen watching. Soon, the creature, though injured, gathered enough strength to became enraged and defensive as it began spewing tiny fractured bolts of electricity.

Reed looked at his sister. "I think whatever this thing is, it's very angry with us, and it's either trying to send us a warning or some kind of message."

"Or punishment." Evelyn pulled the ribbon from her hair and held it in front of the small creature, who settled down almost hypnotically as it swayed in front of the ribbon. It was clear that the creature had been hurt and would need time to recover. "I think we should let Natturia or Sampion know about this. If this is a pixie, we'd better find out how best to handle the situation."

"I know, but I want to watch it for a while. Who knows when I'll get a chance to see it again up close."

"You won't want to! Once the pixies hear about what happened, that we have one of their flying friends trapped, we might be in a lot of trouble with them! Don't you remember what the fairies said pixies are capable of? They can cause us a lot of harm if they work together, and I don't want to be in the path of their wrath."

At that instant, Reed thought back to the fairy photograph. Would the fairies or pixies know that he had it, and would holding a possible pixie hostage help or hurt their situation? "First of all, let's find out if this is a pixie or not. Think about it, Evelyn. If it were an actual pixie, then it'd be able to simply disappear and reappear wherever it wanted to. I also think you're making a bigger deal about the whole situation than you need to. It's probably some kind of bug we've never seen before."

"It doesn't resemble any bug I've seen before, and we've seen a ton since we've moved to the country." Evelyn took yet another careful head-to-toe examination of the minute creature. "I mean, it looks like it has a face . . . sorta . . . like a very small human's!"

It was very hard, indeed, to tell that it was a pixie. After all, it had been damaged in its capture and the seething anger this creature held surely distorted its usual appearance.

"I'm sure that whatever this is, it looked much different before it was injured. We'll want to give it time to not only calm down, but also recuperate. What do you think we should do, Reed?"

"I can't wait to hear what Natturia and Sampion have to say about this! We can make sure this thing doesn't escape the glass jar with either a heavy book to weigh the jar in its place, or we can move the jar and put this creature in a box."

Reed was faced with a bit of a quandary. He didn't want the fairies at their house, especially since he hadn't yet divulged to Evelyn that he'd retrieved his fairy photo. They might know that the photo wasn't destroyed.

"Evelyn, I need to tell you something. Now hear me out. We've been so busy today with the horse farm and looking at pixies that I forgot to tell you that I found the picture."

Evelyn immediately grew incensed that he had not only gone behind her back but was less than honest with her.

"I'm sorry that I went to your room without permission, but the way I see it is that one photo is mine, and I had a right to get it out of your room because I was the one who took it in the first place. Besides, you know how much I've wanted to learn about the fairies and the pixies."

Although Evelyn was fuming, she felt torn. She hoped the fairies would give Reed what he deserved for taking the picture from her room. "You'll have to deal with any consequences if the fairies find out that you have that picture. I won't tell them, but I won't stand behind you either. Now let's summon Natturia and Sampion. Do you remember how?"

"Yes," he said, although he had a very hard time concentrating. He could hardly keep his heart open and his mind on the fairies. Evelyn realized why the summoning wasn't working, and she couldn't help but give Reed a dirty look, as he had cast such a dark feeling over them by stealing the photo back. They agreed to instead head to the pine forest to find the fairies since the faster method had failed.

They secured their captive under a mason jar with a heavy book to weigh it down.

"We also need to cover this entire desk area with one of your shirts or a blanket, Reed, in case Mom or Dad come into your room while we're gone." They did just that, and with the diminutive and mysterious creature hidden and secured, the kids set out to the pine woods to see if they could find Natturia or Sampion.

The Captive

Softly entering the woods while looking up and down each tree, Evelyn and Reed also searched around the ground and behind the small sticks.

"Reed, let's just find a spot and wait for them. They shouldn't take long to appear. Besides, I think I'm able to focus more," Evelyn said hopefully.

As it turned out, it wasn't long before two fairies came into view, except these fairies were not Natturia or Sampion. About ten yards away, halfway up a pine tree, two small figures were giggling and playing tag, chasing and laughing, fluttering around, and darting in and out of the area. Each of these fairies, too, had a fluorescent glow around the soft colors they emitted, which lit up the immediate area. One of the fairies had a shade of brown skin with long, flowing red hair, and a full-length pink gown that waved as it moved around under a dark green sash. The opposing fairy had shorter, light blue hair, a pinkish quality to his skin, and protective weaponry on his back. Shortly, several other fairies joined in the fun, each bringing a variety of soft colors to the immediate area, and as they moved so quickly in every direction, Reed could not help but think that a small, rainbow-colored cloud had appeared and drifted closer toward them. Evelyn and Reed became so caught up watching the fairies frolic for the first time, they almost forgot why they had come to the pine woods, when Evelyn, thinking of their recent capture, summoned enough nerve to speak.

"See, I told you that if you're quiet and wait long enough, you become a part of the forest, and things start happening," Reed whispered as he leaned in toward his sister.

"Excuse me," Evelyn interrupted quietly, so as not to startle the joyous fairies. Immediately, each fairy froze and then turned slowly toward Evelyn and Reed.

One of the beautiful fairies fluttered down toward the children, saying in a quiet, small, high-pitched voice, "You must be Evelyn, and you must be Reed. We have heard much about you."

"Hello," Reed said, awestruck. His eyes were wide as

he and Evelyn stood before the fairies. "Um, are Natturia or Sampion around?"

"We can summon them if that is what you'd like. Don't you want to speak to us? Maybe you want to join our game of tag?" The fairies all giggled at the idea.

"We have another issue we have to speak to them about." Evelyn thought back to the injured creature they'd left on Reed's desk and appealed to the colorful crew of fairies. "If you could hurry, we have to get back soon."

"What can we help you with?" the familiar-sounding voices behind Evelyn and Reed asked simultaneously as they hovered and looked down toward the human pair. "It sounds like a pressing matter."

"We think it is. Our family visited the horse farm earlier today, and when we got home, Reed showed me that he'd captured something we think might be a pixie."

"Oh, dear." Natturia looked at Sampion with a solemn face. "Do you have him secured? I mean, he can't get away, can he?"

Reed was confident that their captive was home safely under the mason jar. "It got hurt pretty badly. We don't know how to help it . . . or if we should help."

"We don't want to risk offending the fairies if we do help it," Evelyn said, urging them to hurry.

"We appreciate your thoughtfulness, Evelyn. You two

return home, and we will meet you there shortly. Sampion and I will confer with Ashkin regarding the next steps if your captive is indeed a pixie. On the other hand, if it is one of our beloved insect friends, then we can likely help it return to its natural home to recover quickly."

Before turning to walk home, Evelyn and Reed took one last look at the rainbow of colors floating around. The unique experience was quickly tucked back into their minds to be relished later as they hastened home. Neither wanted to let any more time pass with the creature in Reed's room unattended.

"You know, Evelyn, because I'm younger than you, it seems that I always have to take a back seat and let you make the decisions. You're the one who talks first, you're the one who gets to meet the fairies first, and you're the one who makes most of the decisions."

"What's your point?"

"Well, I'm the one who found that pixie or whatever it is, and I think any decision about him should be left up to me."

Evelyn stopped in her tracks and turned to look Reed square in the eye. "You are not serious, Reed. You think just because you nabbed that creature at the horse farm, you should be the only one who makes decisions about it? Is that what you're saying?" She walked ahead, not waiting for Reed to answer. All she could think about now was what Reed might do with the creature.

"Can't you see things from my viewpoint, Evvie?"

"I'm not going to talk about it anymore. I think we'd better get back to your room before Natturia and Sampion."

"Of course. You're right again." Reed hated saying it, but he didn't want the fairies to be at his home with the picture still in his journal.

Returning to his desk, he told himself that he would return to this argument when the time was right. For now, the children set aside their dispute to focus on their captive, who lay coughing and twitching, still looking quite hurt, doubled over slightly holding his belly. They could see that one of the wings appeared bent beyond repair.

Natturia and Sampion arrived, fluttering near the children's ears as they all looked down and studied the creature with his ailments.

"Yes, Evelyn and Reed, it looks like you have, indeed, managed to capture a pixie. Do you see his dull coloring? Usually, pixies come in drab colors partly because they enjoy dirt and partly to keep themselves concealed as they cause mischief. One will never find a pixie smiling. They offer, instead, a typical expression of scorn as can be seen in this captive. Most importantly, pixies have magical powers, but they are rarely used for the good of others."

"If they're magical, why didn't this pixie just disappear so that he wasn't captured?" Evelyn inquired.

"You probably surprised him, and it is likely he cannot use any of his powers because he was injured," suggested Sampion.

"What happens to him if we help him recover?" Reed asked. "Do the pixies go back to their ways of causing problems for people?"

"I'm afraid that is the nature of the beast," Natturia said. "I know that they won't ever change completely." She paused. "But we fairies must make sure that they don't unite to take away our pine woods, something they have been trying to do for years. Remember, that's why we enlisted your help."

"If we help this pixie recover, don't you think that the other pixies would appreciate it and be less of a problem for you? I mean, why would they try to take your home from you after you've helped to heal one of their own?" Evelyn struggled to understand.

"It is difficult to explain," Natturia said flatly. "While fairies view life with positive thoughts and energy, pixies have chosen to contribute to mischief. One pixie might use its magical powers, for example, to steal, or another might be good at hiding the things others take enjoyment in."

"Another pixie could be good at conjuring weather

misdeeds or perhaps finding ways to use food to wreak havoc with your meals," added Sampion.

Evelyn and Reed understood, but with more understanding came more questions.

"I don't think we'll ever see the day when pixies will stop being jealous of fairies," Sampion concluded.

Evelyn looked at Reed. "I guess jealousy is common to all forms of life. I just wish people could find happiness in themselves with whatever gifts they have to offer. I suppose we increased our chances of running into a pixie by visiting the horse farm." She set her hand on the hair ribbon, knowing it may have attracted the pixie, which made her feel somewhat responsible for his injury. She didn't like to see anyone or anything in misery, no matter its background. "What can we do to help this pixie?"

"Ashkin, our leader, has given us permission to attend to his injuries and help him heal. We risk attack by any number of pixies if you leave the room, so please stay while we administer aid." Sampion held one of Natturia's hands while his other hand carried the sharply pointed staff for protection. The fairies joined their energy to cast their powers in healing the pixie, who slowly stretched his renewed wings. The kids could see his wings were smaller and considerably less ornate than a fairy's, and his body unfolded fully, strengthening. His tiny eyes opened, squinting with the light of the room, and he stood to face the small audience that looked back. He lacked much of the beauty that the fairies possessed.

Evelyn turned to Reed and then the fairies. "I can see why one would mistake a pixie for a large bug, and this guy doesn't look very happy."

"I'm not happy!" shouted the pixie. "You took away my powers, and now you have threatened to alienate me from the pixie empire. They will surely not allow me back home now that I've been exposed to *you*." The pixie buried his face in his hands and began to sob. "I'll never be able to go back again."

"Why not?" Reed looked seriously at the pixie. "You look fine to me."

"I look fine, but the pixies will know that I've been contaminated by the fairies." Sampion explained to the kids that when the fairies helped the pixie, it created a faint aura that would remain around him.

"What's your name?" Reed asked warily.

"I'm not supposed to tell you," the creature said flatly. After a long pause, he continued, "Since there's no chance of the pixies ever welcoming me back, I might as well." The tiny figure paused as he stood, defeated, with shoulders sunken. "My name is Artemis."

"This is my sister, Evelyn, and my name is Reed," Reed

said, looking up at the fairies, wondering whether to introduce them as well, but Artemis interrupted.

"I know who they are."

"You do?" Evelyn asked, surprised.

"Every pixie knows all the fairies by name. After all,
each pixie has been assigned to a fairy so that we're better
able to eventually conquer them one day; we have to know
each one well," Artemis explained. He shook his head as
he looked down. "I don't know why I'm telling you all this,
but then again, I don't know if it'd make a difference. Can't
you help me?" he pleaded. "I don't know where I'm going
to live now that I've clearly been in contact with a fairy."

Natturia looked very serious. "We will talk more with
our leaders soon. Surely, any pixie knows that one will
have to earn its way out of banishment from either the
clan of fairies or the clan of pixies." Natturia turned and
looked down to Artemis. "You are not the first pixie in all
our years of existence to be expelled."

Evelyn looked at Sampion. "Will Artemis go with you
now?"

"Yes, he will be presented to the Fairy Council while
he proves that he can be trusted and turn his pixie ways
to those more like a fairy. He must know that his choices
are few, as the pixie clan won't have him back readily, and
unless he begins to adopt some of the fairy ways, he won't

be allowed with them either."

Natturia and Sampion turned to leave. "You can meet us back near the pine woods next to the large knotty oak tree tomorrow. For now, we have to process him," Sampion did not wait for a reply.

The fairies quickly disappeared, holding Artemis between them.

Back at the knotty oak tree outside the pine woods, Natturia and Sampion entered with Artemis in tow through a small door that had mysteriously appeared at the base of the tree trunk. The door swiftly slid open, then closed behind them and vanished from view as quickly as it first appeared. Artemis's arms were firmly in the grasp of the fairies as they flew up through the levels inside the hollowed-out tree trunk. When they finally arrived to a south-side room inside the tree, several fairies fluttered above various worms that had burrowed additional space for new captives. Another well-lit room contained a small table and a high semicircular table with three empty high-backed armchairs chairs behind it. The fairies sat at a smaller table while Artemis awaited his fate.

A few minutes seemed like hours to Artemis as he waited to go through this process, having no idea what to expect regarding his future. He watched the fairies whisper to each other for a few moments when they stood and bowed their heads to the entering council members. The council arrived shortly after, and they motioned for Artemis to sit down at his table, which was in front of the council's table. The three council members stood regally with long, brilliant cloaks before gliding into their seats and staring at Artemis, who sat looking powerless, an unusual feeling for one who had spent his entire life thinking up ways to cause problems for others.

A small finch, who acted as a bailiff for the courtroom, sat at the bottom of the council's high desk, looking at the pixie and then back to the council. After a moment, a screen on the wall of the tree opened, and the view outside the tree showed two, then three large crows flying toward the treetop. Soon there were two more birds, followed by a group of four. It was clear that they were being summoned, as soon there were forty crows flying, and within five minutes, close to a hundred crows gathered on the top branches of the tree, each carrying a fairy. Artemis watched in fascination, but he also grew more nervous. More crows flew around the treetops, moving in independent directions and making the sky dark. Word had gotten out that the fairies were holding a pixie captive—a rare occurrence—and the fairies, many of whom had hitched rides on the crows, were anxious to see for themselves. What would the pixies do once they heard that the fairies had captured one of their own? The fairies dismounted their winged carriers before each bird rested on another tree until needed later. In the meantime, the blackbirds' specialty was to be on alert and signal to others whenever trouble was near.

Inside the oak tree, the prisoner processing began. The finch read aloud the charges being brought against Artemis once the courtroom quieted down.

"I understand that your name is Artemis. We are the council members who will evaluate your case and determine whether or not you can be rehabilitated. At the very least, you helping us with our daily tasks involving nature would be expected. Over time, you would regain some of your powers, but only if you abide by our rules and try your best to comply. We know from experience that pixies cannot be completely reformed, but we are always hopeful that there will be an exception to that rule."

A slower-moving council member addressed Artemis next. "First and foremost, do you desire to be reformed? We cannot help any pixie that does not at least desire to change."

Artemis thought for a long moment. "I don't know that I have any choice in the matter. If I return to the pixies, they'll surely disown me because I've been tainted, and I need a home."

The third council member asked in a higher-pitched and softer tone, "What sort of pixie mischief was your specialty?"

"My specialty was breaking items and then reassembling them." Immediately after Artemis spoke, the finch squawked, as it detected Artemis was not being truthful.

"Oh my. It looks like you are not having a good start, Artemis."

"I'm sorry. It's just that I've heard the punishment is less for breaking things than it is for other crimes. It's hard to change old habits just like that." Artemis snapped his fingers for effect. "I will try–little by little. Just give me a chance," he pleaded. "My specialty was to hide things and then make them reappear elsewhere. It was such fun to watch people look around for their missing items." Artemis chuckled. "We would hide things so often on some people that they actually thought they were losing their minds." He laughed and then quickly composed himself.

"Artemis, we know that pixies don't think kindly of fairies," explained one of the council members, "and that they are jealous of all the fairy virtues. You forget that we, too, have been exposed to many of the pixies' pranks over time, and we have worked hard to uphold much of the fairies' accomplishments and advancements.

"The bottom line is that you will have to make amends

for many—though not every—offense made against the Gunderson family. We have discussed the matter at length and made a special selection of the crimes you'll atone for.

"You will start by working with the worms. After they approve the work you've done, then you can help some of our bird friends with their tasks. After three weeks have passed, we will meet again to discuss your progress. Once you learn to love and enjoy the life of a fairy, you will see how much of this world is filled with beauty and kindness."

Artemis agreed reluctantly and left with his head bowed. He had spent all his life making life more difficult for others, and he didn't see how not being a mischief-maker was going to be any fun. In fact, he thought that life would be downright boring without a laugh here or there at someone else's expense.

He was brought to his holding room, where he was provided necessary comforts. He kept his room dark and cried with despair at the enormous change in life. He set out to hold on to what little hope he could find in his heart and tried to see something positive in his situation.

Artemis began by helping the worms work—a job he would surely detest. He hated them, and he couldn't think of how to be happy helping worms, much less fairies.

The work supervisor, an oversized grub with a

camel-colored shelled head, a soft creamy body within a translucent casing, and sharp teeth, gave instructions to the new captive, sounding as if he had administered them many times before.

Speaking with large incisors that caused a speech impediment, he directed Artemis, "Now that you've aw-wived at ower fathility, you will help usth to make ower dwellings even larger. You will be weethponthible for thith shovel ithsued to you, and make sure to note itsth condition before you thstart using it. Any damage you cauzth to thith ithsued tool or any other fairwee pwop-erty will wethult in additional work time to pay fow the damage. Capeesh?" The grub's scratchy, low voice made Artemis uncomfortable, and he nodded and tried his best to overlook the impediment and focus on the instruc-tions. Yes, Artemis did indeed "capeesh" and understood even more as he watched the worms crawl to the work area and begin gnawing on the wood to be removed, to clear a room in this knotty area of the tree. As the worms gnawed, a fine sawdust began to mount.

"Well, start shoveling," one of the worms directed sternly.

Befuddled, Artemis slowly started to shovel the pile of sawdust, but the question now was where to put the sawdust once it was picked up. Seeing Artemis wander around aimlessly with a full shovel, another worm direct-ed softly, "You have to bring the sawdust to the tree entry, where the large beetles will pick it up to be recycled and used to heat the homes of our nature friends."

Artemis nodded, thankful to receive directions, and quickly caught on. Before long, he could see that the room had been hollowed out, leaving only the tasks of sweeping and sanding down any remaining rough patches. As he looked around, he couldn't believe the job he had original-ly thought to be huge was already complete.

A nearby worm commented, "Haven't you ever heard the saying 'Many hands makes light work'?"

Artemis, of course, had never heard the proverb before because some pixies had never had to work; they always found ways to get out of it by deflecting tasks to other pixies who were not as clever. Artemis also noticed that he really didn't mind doing work, especially when there was so many others helping to get the job done. In fact, he liked it and couldn't help but feel a bit of accomplishment, and after two weeks on the job, he had become quite ef-ficient.

"Okay, what else needs to be done?" he asked with sincere eagerness.

The supervisor looked pleased at Artemis's job perfor-mance and his attitude. "Now you are ready to help our bird friends. You'll move to an outdoor location, where you will find a red-winged blackbird waiting for your arrival. He'll give you your next set of instructions."

Artemis actually enjoyed the new sights and experiences, which he found helped pass time quickly, and he was totally unaware of how his admiration for the fairies was increasing. For so long, he had been caught up in being unruly and playing tricks on others, never taking time to imagine doing anything else, and of course, pixies never would have allowed him to be helpful. Advancing in importance was something else he had never experienced, and he noticed he was beginning to feel an odd way he couldn't recognize.

Standing before the council again, he listened carefully. "We have been informed that you are performing your duties quite well, Artemis, and we are proud of how well you are helping with the tasks that we've assigned you. We want to challenge you to help humans. Of course, you'll start out with a small task, and in return, we will allow you use of your powers in a restricted capacity and under supervised conditions for now." His outlook and trustworthiness had improved to the point that he was now going to be assigned tasks to help humans. *Help humans. Me? Me helping humans. I sort of like that,* he thought.

"We have human friends who have moved to the area,"

another council continued, "and they have proven their kindness to the fairies; we will help them in return. Think back to the young boy in the family and the special toy that brings him joy. Let's see what you can do to make up for the pixies' misdeed committed against the boy named Reed."

Artemis had been so accustomed to devising countless pranks that he'd never thought helping a human would be worthwhile. It had been more fun for him to play around with the subject of their pranks. He had these strange positive feelings now, but he also had feelings of wanting revenge on Reed, who had captured him in the first place, and he could never forget the day that he had been swatted, damaged, and turned in to the fairies. Dismal as it seemed, there was no alternative. He'd have to put aside those thoughts of getting back at Reed and help him.

It might not be so tough–he sort of liked the having a new responsibility. He wasn't being goaded by the other pixies into joining mischievous actions. For the first time, he had an opportunity to shine, and he rather liked the prospect.

While Artemis was gone, the Gundersons had started school, and both Evelyn and Reed quickly established after-school routines. Reed's time was spent first snacking and then letting off the excess energy that had accumulated after sitting in class. Artemis watched the Gunderson household from a distance, gradually gaining closer views, each day passing without incident. It was rather easy for Artemis to pick up on Reed's schedule and routines, either playing outside with his friend or in the woods, and finding the space glider left unattended in Reed's room was a cinch.

On the back closet shelves that cut through the lower portion of his closet, the toy was placed with obvious importance, as it had an entire small shelf to itself. Artemis walked around the front of the toy and then viewed it from behind, standing with his hand on his chin, thinking of ways that he could atone for hiding it repeatedly when Reed most wanted to use it. With a wave of his hand, he transformed the glider to be made of a sturdier material than the original thin plastic, and he put a homing device inside the engine compartment that would beep after being thrown. To test his newly acquired magic, Artemis propelled the glider across the room, where it immediately began to beep until it was picked up.

Artemis returned later in the day to watch Reed's reaction as he played in the backyard with his glider.

* * *

Like clockwork, Reed came home from school starving and eager to start playing with his favorite friend. He grabbed a banana and a cookie, announcing to Evelyn,

"I'll be in the backyard playing with my glider for a while before I have to do my homework. Rupert's coming along."

He didn't noticed the changes to his toy until he propelled it straight ahead. It felt heavier than he'd recalled, and it flew well beyond the property line, then up higher, doing two loop-de-loops before finally resting in the tall grass next to the yard.

Rupert barked at the glider while it beeped repeatedly in the tall grass.

"Rupert! Did you see that? Wow! This glider never flew that far before, and that's the first loop-de-loop ever!"

Reed was so proud of his new accomplishment, he didn't notice the glider beeping until he picked it up. "Hmm. I must have triggered a switch. I didn't know that was there before."

Artemis smiled his broad, crooked, raggedy grin as he watched from a high tree branch at his success with this first atonement task, and he thought the addition of the homing device on Reed's toy was a brilliant idea. He fluttered behind tree branches, watching.

Another easy fix was Evelyn's favorite necklace, which he and his fellow pixies had hidden just after they'd stashed Reed's glider. The gold necklace with a small birthstone had particular sentimental value, as Evelyn's grandmother had given it to her.

Artemis lifted the lid of the jewelry box and found the necklace in a center compartment. Pulling it out, he stretched it across the top of the bureau to get a better look at it. He decided to enhance the dull necklace chain with a thicker sparkling gold chain, a larger birthstone, and a stronger clasp. Surely, Evelyn would appreciate the upgraded beauty.

He was not only thrilled to get some of his magical powers back, he also noticed his heart felt a little more satisfied. It had been a whole new experience that he would not soon forget.

Quickly, though, the fact that he would never return to the life he had known with the pixies flashed through his mind and made him angry. He began to wish for ways to return to the pixies; after all, he missed them greatly.

"Hrrmmph, I wish I could get back home; I do not like being here," he muttered. He felt confused to be filled with satisfaction one moment, and disgust and uncertainty the next. The fluctuating emotions made him angrier. He spoke softly at first to himself. "I'll have to reach deeper to move on. I will triumph!"

It was time to see what the Fairy Council had in store for him next. Artemis told himself that he was not going to wait to get out of his imprisonment, but he also knew that he would have to acquire more of his magical powers before he could escape. When he was back in his holding cell, he hung his head in deep thought, strategizing his pixie return and resolving to become stronger, daring, craftier, and more resourceful than he had been before his capture.

9.

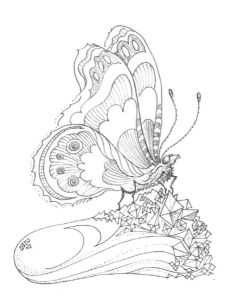

Kindred Conflict

The fairies eagerly carried out their seasonal duties every year, preparing for the arrival of fall, since the cold winter months required them to primarily dwell underground. Making sure that nature smoothly made the transition from summer to fall was an enormous task, and it required cooperation, focused work, and hyper-coordination, but it was an exciting responsibility. Securing homes for animals, completing the fall harvest, and watching all of nature's colorful passages made for an incredibly busy but thrilling time for the fairies.

At the council headquarters, the fairy leaders were busy seeing to any conflicts or snags in the transition. They also held another council meeting to address Artemis's reparations.

"Artemis, after reading about your progress and the ways you've helped Reed and Evelyn thus far, we think that you are, indeed, ready to progress in your journey. We want you to help the Gunderson children with a particular focus on making more complex atonements for the misdeeds committed against them. Specifically, we've provided you a list of some of the pranks you and the other pixies performed; you are required to make reparations by helping the family. How you choose to complete the required tasks is up to you as is whether or not you reveal yourself to the parents. We understand that . . . let's see . . ." The council leader paused, referring to the folder containing Artemis's case information. "Apparently, you have already revealed yourself to the children."

"The Gunderson children have seen me, and they know my identity because one of them smacked me in the face. He made me fall to the ground, and then he pinched my back and almost ruined my wings." Artemis tried not to sound too indignant, but he recalled the capture vividly, and his anger was in danger of bubbling to the surface. To quickly curtail any outward tension, he smiled broadly and agreed to be of service to the family again with plea-sure. He didn't want the fairies to have the slightest suspi-cion otherwise, and he was confident that he could hold a positive outward appearance despite suddenly feeling very vengeful on the inside. He was eager to strengthen his magical powers as soon as possible.

* * *

Evelyn and Reed were well into their school year, in a solid daily routine of returning home, letting Rupert out-side for a romp, and chatting in the kitchen about their daily highlights while chomping down snacks as warm sunlight streamed in through the windows. Today they discussed encounters with friends, school projects to be worked on, and their teachers.

"What do you think you're going to do for your sci-ence project, Reed?"

"I'm seriously thinking about doing something with baking since you've told me a million times that baking is science, and I get to eat my experiments! You're the bak-ing master, so I thought that I'd get some insider tips from our resident expert."

"Me?" Evelyn couldn't help but blush a little. "I can only help you if you plan ahead, if I have extra time, and you do most of the work. I have more schoolwork than ever before, so I'm limited with how much help I can give you."

"Thank you, Evvie! I'll go to my bedroom to get the guidelines for the science project; I'll be right back." Reed raced upstairs to get the assignment from his backpack and then ran downstairs. As he looked up after reaching the last step, he quickly slowed to a walk, all the while keeping his eye fixated on the hovering pixie in front of him.

"I can help with your science project, too, Reed," Artemis offered. Reed gaped at the small figure whose appearance was now quite different. Artemis was no longer covered in dirt, carrying crumpled wings on his back, with a doubled-up body or ruffled hair. He not only looked cleaner, he also looked stronger, and his wings seemed fully repaired, although he still had the drably colored, gnarly pixie characteristics. Besides his improved physical characteristics, his willing attitude and tone enhanced his overall appearance.

"Hey, aren't you that pixie I caught a while ago? You look so . . ." Reed struggled to find a description to define Artemis's new look. "Well, you sure don't look so dirty and nasty. You seem happier and well . . . pleasant!"

"Indeed, I am that pixie, and I'm here to help you out in any way that I can," he replied.

"Wow. I'm shocked that you'd even offer to help. Evelyn and I did a lot of research on fairies and pixies, you know, and we learned that helping is not on a pixie's to-do list! You'd much rather cause problems and have a big laugh about it. I'm more shocked that you're even talking to me. I'd think that after I swatted you, you'd want nothing to do with me. Even though the whole thing was an accident. I mean, really–wouldn't you want to do something to hurt me back?"

"That was the old me," Artemis said, trying to sound convincing. "The fairies have had me working to make amends for some of the tricks I played, and so far, I've proven to them that I can behave more like a fairy. They've even allowed me limited access to my magical powers–just as long as I use them for good, of course." Artemis couldn't help but feel a little conflicted–he was making progress toward regaining his freedom, but the question of where he would reside once he had successfully completed his time working for the fairies remained in the back of his mind, and his allegiance to the pixies had not yet been fully erased. The uncertainty about his future lingered like the smell of pungent Limburger cheese–one of his favorite treats.

Reed listened but he didn't believe a word Artemis said. Maybe it was because Reed had observed too many of his classmates saying they'd changed after acting up in school, and they'd end up doing the same disruptions over and over.

"Okay, Artemis, what are you supposed to do for me?"

"I'm at your service. Do you need help with school? Friends? Homework? Or maybe you need help getting along with your sister or your parents. The fairies gave me a list of seven atonements that they require of me, but anything else I help you with will be a bonus for both of us."

Everybody deserves a second chance, Reed thought, looking upward in deep thought, with his forefinger and thumb supporting his chin, as he tried to come up with a way that Artemis could help. It didn't take long before the jealous feelings of playing second fiddle to Evelyn crept into his mind. True, she was older, but Reed felt the number of times she had been first at something far outnumbered the chances he had gotten to do the same, and that simply wasn't fair. He'd had enough of it. Sure, he knew he was being a little petty, but he didn't know how to be rid of the jealousy. It seemed that Evelyn was always better than he was, and he didn't like her being the only one who made decisions. She'd appeared to grab the spotlight with the fairies when Reed's interest in them was considerably higher. Now was a perfect opportunity to outshine Evelyn with Artemis's help. She didn't have to know about

Artemis's reappearance–not just yet–and Reed liked holding the reins for once.

"Hmm . . . let me see. I have a science experiment for school that you can help me with. I'd really like to have you to myself for the time being. You don't need to let Evelyn know that you're helping me or even that you're here at our house for now, so let's just keep this between you and me." Reed loved being in control and knowing something important that Evelyn didn't, although keeping secrets from his family created a feeling of unease that he couldn't seem to shake. "Let's go back to my room where we can talk in private."

They returned to Reed's room, where he shut the door behind them.

"Before we start on my science project, can you first help me clean my room quickly? Then maybe you can help me with a fort outside that I've been wanting to make. I haven't been able to really get started with it since my dad's been busy. If I could build that before the snow falls, then I wouldn't have to deal with the snow or wait until spring, and a fort would give me another place to get away from my sister. And nope, she won't be invited in."

"I could do that easily, although the fairies expect me to help Evelyn as well. Let's start with your room first." With a wave of Artemis's hands, Reed's room was immaculate, and Artemis looked back to see Reed's reaction. He was taken aback somewhat at how quickly he'd accomplished this request with his magical powers. Was this temporary, something to do with the fairies who'd allowed him to use these powers, or was it because he'd used them to help rather than cause mischief?

"Nice! That's so cool! Evelyn will be surprised I was able to get my room clean so fast! Now, can we go outside to work on my fort? We can start on my science project later."

"Certainly. I'll wait outside for you."

Reed went downstairs and put on his jacket, walking past the kitchen without saying anything to Evelyn, who was doing her homework at the kitchen counter.

Reed's footsteps caught her attention. How odd it seemed that he wouldn't say anything to her. She paused her studies for a moment as she watched him leave through the back door. She followed quietly behind him, watching him leave the back patio, disappear behind the nearby shrubbery, and head to the other side of the back-yard before she blurted, "Where are you going, Reed, and who were you talking to?"

"Oh, hi, Evelyn. Uh . . . I'm just talking to myself. I already cleaned my room, so I thought that I'd come out here and think of where to build my fort before it gets too dark."

"You already cleaned your room? In less than five minutes? Your room looked like a hurricane went through it! You know if it's not up to Mom and Dad's standards . . . well, you'll just have to answer to them, and you know that you're supposed to get your homework done first before anything else."

Reed rolled his eyes. "I'm well aware of the rules. I won't be out here long, and I'll have plenty of time to tackle my homework tonight. Now good-bye. I want to be alone so I can concentrate on the details of my fort; I'd like to get it done before winter comes."

"Fine. You know what you're doing, and you'll have to face the consequences for any poor decisions you make."

Evelyn abruptly shut the door, but she couldn't shrug off her suspicion that Reed wasn't being completely open with her. She also couldn't help but notice the increasing tension between them. That was definitely out of the ordinary; it left a most unpleasant feeling, as if a dark cloud hung above her.

Outside, Reed waited to make sure that Evelyn was well out of sight before continuing his conversation with Artemis, who'd quietly waited behind the door. Reed made every attempt to ignore his stomach, which was beginning to feel a little sour. He wasn't sure if it was something he'd eaten at school or the feeling of not being forthright with his sister. Being anything less than completely honest with her was gnawing at him more than he'd expected.

He went forth with his plans and didn't want to waste any of the time he had with Artemis to himself. "I'd like the fort fairly close; I don't want to trudge too far from the house in the wintertime, although I know my parents won't like it too close to the house. Let me think a little more about the perfect location." Reed put his hands on his waist and surveyed the backyard. "Hey, how about we build the fort just behind those weeds at the end of our property? It can go right behind those branches of the tree that's on the corner of our lot. I can't think of why my parents would mind it being there, and there's no one building on the lot behind our house for a long time."

"You've got it. How big would you like it, and how do you want the interior to look? What other–"

Before Artemis could finish, Evelyn walked around the side of the house. "I knew it! I just heard you talking to Artemis! I knew you were up to something."

"So what? He's helping me because he said the fairies are having him make right for the tricks the pixies played, and because I saw him first, he's working on a couple of things I want his help with. When he's done, you can have him, but only when I'm good and ready."

"You go right ahead. I'll just wait and watch to see what trick he has up his sleeve for you. Remember what Shakespeare said: 'A leopard cannot change his spots.'" Evelyn turned to go back into the kitchen to sort out her feelings. Was she feeling left out, or was she angry about the way Reed had just treated her? Maybe she was hurt that Reed didn't want her opinion as he had so often before.

What hurt Evelyn most was that Reed felt he had to keep something from her. Of course, she had recently done the same by not sharing her first encounter with Natturia and Sampion. But was that really the same kind of transgression? She had taken pride that she and Reed were particularly close as siblings went and that they'd always had complete trust in one another. Now it seemed like he was going behind her back. Regaining her concentration on her schoolwork took more effort than usual. The chair in the kitchen felt cold, the room felt uninviting, and her mind could think of nothing else but her brother and what he and Artemis were up to. She sincerely did not want Artemis to do anything to damage the solid relationship she and Reed shared, nor did she want Artemis to cause any trouble for her brother–though she told herself that Reed was certainly old enough to face whatever consequences his actions brought.

All she could focus on now was the feeling of deceit. But what had changed, and why had Reed planned to keep Artemis's return a secret from her? Did Artemis recommend it, or was the decision entirely up to Reed? The answer didn't particularly matter to Evelyn as much as being at odds with her brother. It felt so isolating, especially when there weren't a lot of friends living nearby to turn to. The possibility of discussing her alienation from Reed with her new fairy friends popped in her head, as did the photograph of the fairies. With Artemis back on the scene, she didn't want to risk that picture getting into the wrong hands, knowing that the pixies and fairies were at such odds. Her mind wandered to all sorts of possibilities, one of which was the public learning of the fairies' existence; she was sure mayhem would break out soon after.

At that point, she was compelled to turn to Natturia and Sampion for answers in helping her cope. They'd possibly see things more objectively than she could, and they might even offer solutions. She cleared her mind and focused on her fairy friends, whom she summoned in short order; within seconds, they were standing on the kitchen counter.

"Oh, thank you for coming so quickly, Natturia and Sampion. I've got a problem that I'm not sure how to handle—particularly because it involves Reed."

"You look alarmed, Evelyn," Sampion noticed.

"I'm sorry to bother you, but Reed just isn't himself. It fortunately doesn't happen very often, but we don't seem to be getting along well at the moment. He actually went as far as not telling me that he's interacting with Artemis. We usually share everything—especially when it involves either fairies or pixies, and I'm very worried about the photograph of the fairy birth—I know Reed still has it."

"Oh, dear. That's not good news at all." Natturia looked at Sampion with deep concern. "I'm afraid that he'll take advantage of Artemis to spite me and perhaps jeopardize any progress Artemis has made with the fairies. Besides, I think Reed will get in trouble with our parents if Artemis goes ahead and helps him build the fort he wants."

Natturia assured Evelyn that she was wise to notify the fairies for Artemis's sake and his progress in making amends, and for the future and safety of the fairies. "We surely don't want Reed to build on any other area that we fairies find sacred, but we know how we can help."

They agreed that Artemis's journey to make up for previous mischief was still fairly new, and they wanted him to stay on the path to success.

Sampion stood tall and guarded. "As far as the fort goes, it is sometimes best to learn from making mistakes. We will help you by offering you a choice between a butterfly or a dragonfly to use as your agent so that you can keep an eye on Reed and Artemis and retrieve and destroy the photograph."

"Guys, I really do regret that I didn't convince Reed to destroy the picture right away, and I'm thankful that you'll help. Regarding the agent, I'll pick the butterfly."

"All right, we'll assign the Red Admiral to your case."

"The Red Admiral?" Evelyn wondered if somehow the military would be involved.

Natturia explained that the Red Admiral was a type of regional butterfly that was part of their counterintelligence fleet. "He won't have long to help you, though," she went on, "as most of the wild butterflies have already migrated; we keep a few on our staff as long as possible for special projects."

Sampion added, "Because butterflies are very quiet creatures, they are stealthy. You must know that whenever the Admiral communicates to you, he will lose his scales in the process, so keep your questions important and succinct."

Much of what the fairies told Evelyn about the butterfly spy made sense, and it was not long at all before the flapping of wings against her bedroom window caught her attention.

"Hello there, Admiral!" Evelyn adjusted her window screen to let the butterfly inside, watching him fly softly to the dresser top, where the fairies had stood earlier. The Admiral looked about the room, using his antennae to take in information while flapping his elegant black wings with dotted white patches. It also looked to Evelyn as if Mother Nature had painted an orange-red stripe along one wing and up the other.

The Admiral waited for directions from Evelyn and flittered around, getting a sense of the room. Constantly checking over her shoulders for eavesdropping ears, Evelyn pointed out Reed's room as well as the backyard, where Reed planned on building his fort. Searching the area well helped the butterfly seek out hiding places and an escape route.

After Evelyn and Reed served each other a dinner course of cold shoulder, they returned to their rooms to complete homework and retire in silence, wondering if their sibling felt as miserable as they did. Evelyn could hardly wait until peace returned to the household and wondered if this episode could be chalked up to growing pains. For now, she had to find a comfortable home for the butterfly to rest overnight.

* * *

Outside the next day, Evelyn released the Admiral to survey the work Reed and Artemis were doing in the yard. As the butterfly returned to her bedroom window, Evelyn took out a piece of plain white paper, where the butterfly stood gently moving his wings ever so slightly to lose a few scales to communicate a message. When the colored scales dropped to the white paper, Evelyn could see that they spelled the words *journal* and *magic rock*.

"Hmm, I'll have to figure out why those words are important, Admiral, but right now, I also need you to go to Reed's room while he's outside and find that science journal."

The Admiral performed his duties swiftly, and it did not take long for him to return to show her the location of Reed's journal. She hastily rummaged through it, finding the photograph and sliding it into her back pants pocket. She knew that it wouldn't be long before Reed discovered the picture's removal, and he might even resort to having Artemis take his side. Evelyn simply felt it was her duty to help the fairies, and it was worth taking these chances, as she was essentially helping Reed as well. Something was clearly clouding his judgment, and when given the chance to explain, she was sure he would understand why she'd had to destroy the picture.

* * *

Evelyn looked outside the next morning at sunrise to see a new fort standing at the edge of their property. She was shocked at how quickly it had come together, and she knew that her parents wouldn't be happy with its location. Finding Reed already at the breakfast counter, her dad at the kitchen table reading the morning paper, and her mom making bagged lunches, Evelyn hoped that it wouldn't be considered downright tattling, but she couldn't resist wearing a huge smile and announcing, "I see that you got your fort built, Reed. Congratulations."

Reed pursed his lips. Deep crinkles cut across his forehead as he gave Evelyn eyes that would shoot daggers if they could. He had not yet informed their parents of his new hideaway, and fortunately for Evelyn, he had been

too busy with the fort the night before to check his journal. He wondered why Evelyn had brought it up.

Peering over his newspaper, Mr. Gunderson inquired, "What fort is that, Reed? Oh, and good morning, Evelyn."

Evelyn innocently replied, "Good morning. I saw that Reed had finished building his fort yesterday, and I wanted to congratulate him on it; he's been waiting to build one ever since we moved here."

Both parents looked sternly at Reed, waiting for his explanation. "I was going to surprise you guys and save you some time, Dad. I know that you've been busy working and getting house projects finished," Reed sheepishly explained, although he knew he hadn't received his parents' permission first. He did like how quickly he'd come up with his defense, however.

"Reed! You know you have to ask permission before you decide on a substantial decision like that, and you should think how it would impact others in our family."

Both parents peered out the patio window to get a look at the fort.

"In fact, son, I'm afraid that you'll have to take it down, because it's not altogether on our property," Mr. Gunderson directed. "If you had taken the time to talk with us, we would've made you aware of important information like that."

Mrs. Gunderson added, "The underground watering system is also something I know you didn't even consider. You may have ruptured a watering line, and I don't think you're in a position to cover that cost. The water lines aren't too deep below the ground and can easily be damaged. I sure hope your fort's not in the way of it."

"I didn't know that you had all the wood you needed to build the fort already," Mr. Gunderson continued, "and I can't imagine how you were able to build it so quickly. I'd surely think we would have noticed it going up at some point. We'll have to discuss this more this evening when I get home from work; none of us have the time this morning to get into it."

Reed gave Evelyn another dirty look. "Oh, all right." He hastily finished his breakfast without uttering another word. Evelyn caught the evil glance but went on her way, confident that she had handled the morning the best she could. She went to her room to check on the Admiral before she left for school. As she hurried to get ready for school, she relayed the breakfast episode to the Admiral and directed him to be on guard for any possible revenge plans that Reed may have.

* * *

As soon as Reed returned home from school, he used

Artemis's help to make quick work of tearing down his fort while saving the building material to use at a later date on a location permitted by his parents. Evelyn watched Reed, who was clearly despondent; she knew it was wise to steer clear of him until he was in a better mood, so she turned her attention to how the Admiral was faring.

Perched upon her desk lamp, the butterfly rested until Evelyn returned to her room. The Admiral watched her set a glass of water on her desk, where she was about to tackle homework. Being parched himself, he immediately waggled through the air to the rim of the water glass, where he tried to reach into the interior for a drink. Evelyn watched as she settled into her chair. "Oh no! I didn't even think of setting something out for you to drink, Admiral. A thousand apologies!" She rushed to the bathroom, where she found a small plastic bottle cap next to a brilliant blue rock on the vanity. She filled the cap with water and returned to her bedroom with the plastic cap and blue rock in hand. "Hmm. Reed must have left this rock here." She instantly knew that this could be the rock the Admiral had warned her about the night before. She examined it closely from all sides, as it was the oddest-shaped rock, and it changed color before her eyes, deepening to ever-evolving shades of blue. How curious! The rock, about the size of a tablespoon, had both sharp and smooth edges and got increasingly warm in Evelyn's hand, to the point she could no longer hold it. The burning sensation became intense as the rock glowed a deep crimson, and Evelyn tossed the rock to the floor, where it returned to its original hue.

Reed returned to his room after dismantling the fort and caught a glimpse of Evelyn in her room. He chose to ignore her and walk straight to his room, but as soon as Evelyn heard him shut the door, she heard him rushing to the bathroom and then to her room.

"Did you see my blue rock?" Reed's tone did not invite Evelyn to respond in a pleasant manner, but she fought back the urge to appear negative.

"Yeah, I saw it; you left it in the bathroom. I didn't know what it was, so I picked it up just to get a closer look, and because it started to burn my hand when I held it, I dropped it right there on the floor before you came in." Evelyn pointed to the floor where the mysterious rock fell. "What is that thing, anyways, and where did you get it?"

He moved to the middle of Evelyn's room and picked up the rock, holding it tightly in his hand. "It's a gift from Artemis, and it's none of your business."

Evelyn severely disliked this latest version of Reed, and she so wished that things would return to normal between them. An enormous cloud of sadness enveloped her; she just had to look away from Reed before her tear-flooded eyes began to overflow.

After a few moments, Reed's face warmed as he looked at Evelyn. He blurted out, "Oh, Evelyn. I had no idea how bad you felt, and I'm sorry for the way I've been treating you."

"What makes you think I feel so lousy? Maybe I'm just fine."

"My new rock allows me to read your mind and your heart—at least for a brief moment. I know how bad you feel about how things have been between us lately, and I'm sorry; I really didn't know how deeply my actions hurt you, but I see now. Will you forgive me? I was just upset that you always seem to be the one in charge, and . . ." Reed tried to remember, but he couldn't think how things even got out of hand or why he was really mad at her in the first place. He just knew that he didn't like the feeling of distance with her, and he missed their typical closeness. "Well, I have to talk to Mom and Dad about where I can put my fort later, but maybe you want to help."

"Sorry, Reed; I'm not that interested in forts, but I'd be happy to visit the next one you build. It's just nice to know that I'd be welcome in it. And for what it's worth, I'm sorry, too. I really can't stand it when we're at odds."

Reed turned to call over his shoulder, "Hey, Artemis. All is now A-OK with Evelyn." Artemis flew around the corner of the hall into Evelyn's room with a big smile on his face. "Guess I'll start work on my science project now." And with that, Reed and Artemis set off to the kitchen to get started.

10.

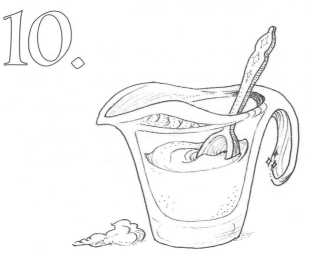

Confronting Complications

In the kitchen, Reed was thumbing through a recipe index when Evelyn joined him. She began to organize her backpack, which rested on a kitchen chair, so she would be fully prepared for school the next day. Now on a more comfortable and cooperative path, Evelyn and Reed put aside their spat and began planning their school science projects. Evelyn also wanted Reed to know more about Artemis's return and felt compelled to tell him that she'd taken back the photograph.

"I'm so glad we're not at odds anymore." She paused before continuing. "I have to confide a couple of things to you. Please just hear me out. It's really important that we don't have any secrets from one another."

"I'm in total agreement with that."

"In that case, I have two things to share with you. The first is that when we weren't getting along, the fairies gave me a butterfly, whom I called Admiral, to help me. I was feeling pretty lonely when we were having our fight."

"You're lucky, or maybe I should say the Admiral is! I almost smashed him when I saw him on the wall in the hallway, but instead, I just picked him up and let him go outside. You say he was helping you?"

"Yeah, the fairies knew how I was feeling, and they sent him to help me. The Admiral informed me where you had your journal . . . and I just had to take back that photograph for the fairies' sake."

"Evelyn! You know how important that picture is to me!" Reed let out a growl. "I didn't even bring my journal out of my room."

"You know that it was just a matter of time before you'd forget that the fairy picture was in your science journal, and it would end up wherever you found the latest and greatest new discovery. Just think of all the things that could end up happening: the picture falls out of the journal onto the floor and someone picks it up, or your teacher checks your science journal and ends up seeing the picture, or you forget to bring your journal to school and Mom or Dad thumb through it—"

"Okay. Okay. I get your point," Reed grumbled, leaning his head on his hands and offering a clear scowl.

Artemis flew into the room and landed on Reed's shoulder. "Why so glum, pal?"

"Oh, it's nothing." Reed looked at Evelyn, not sure if he should disclose the photo to Artemis or not. Wisely, he chose to stay mum.

Evelyn didn't see any benefit to Artemis's return, though she did notice that Artemis looked much improved compared to their initial encounter. "Hello, Artemis. What are your plans today?"

"The fairies are allowing me to make up for the tricks that the pixies played on you and your family." Reluctantly, he added, "I know. I was involved, too, and because I got caught, I need to complete a list of atonements to be released from their captivity." He did not sound at all thrilled about the idea.

"He's not off to a great start, getting you in trouble for building that fort." Evelyn looked straight at Reed.

"That was totally my fault, and I accept full responsibility. Artemis had nothing to do with that decision; he was only helping me with one of my requests."

"One of your requests? How many do you have?"

"I thought I'd ask him to help me out with my science project, but I got sidetracked with the fort." Turning up from his cookbook, Reed felt compelled to share his opinion with Artemis. "You know that everyone in my house has been affected by problems that you and your pixie friends made for us, Artemis, but you made it most difficult for Evelyn."

Artemis was taken aback and had to reflect over the list of tricks that he and the other pixies had played on the family. "I suppose you are referring to the ... what did you call it? Oh yeah–the pastry cake she made. I remember the pixie clan called it the Show Stopping Shenanigan." Artemis tried with all his might not to reveal his amusement at his recollection of the fair judging, but his smirk was all too evident to Reed, who found it quite disrespectful, even if Artemis had been perfectly helpful with Reed's fort earlier. That fair incident, and the horror Evelyn had been through, hoping no one had seen the fairy inside the baked cake after slicing it, came back to Reed quickly and wouldn't soon be forgotten.

Rupert, who had been gnawing quietly on a bone in the family room, entered the kitchen, growling at Artemis.

"It doesn't appear that your pet likes me too much. That's okay. I'm used to it. Here, boy." Artemis quickly tossed a couple pebble-sized doggie treats to the floor in front of Rupert. Rupert, of course, wasted no time in snatching them up and gobbling them down. Then he looked up at Artemis for more.

"For one of my atonement tasks, I'm to help your dog," Artemis announced as he waved his hands amongst a swirl of shimmering luster, revealing a small bag of treats and a large tug-of-war toy for Reed to give Rupert later.

"I suppose, but, Reed, how can we trust a pixie? Don't you remember what he and the other pixies did around our house? My cake was almost a catastrophe, and although he helped you with your fort, he did nothing to stop you from getting in trouble. Don't you think he might change back to his old ways—even a little bit?"

"Of course not," Artemis interjected before Reed had a chance to answer. "The Council of Fairies would have my head, and who knows how long I'd be imprisoned in that old oak tree? I'm getting used to having some of my magic powers back now, and I certainly won't do anything to risk losing them again. Besides, I want to be helpful to you. In fact, Evelyn, I think when you look around the kitchen, you'll find all the dishes put away—where they belong, of course. You'll also find a new-and-improved favorite necklace in your room, and Reed, I believe I've seen your satisfaction with your space glider and with fort construction and deconstruction. Oh, and don't forget one of my recent big helps, Evelyn! Who gave Reed the mind-reading rock, which led to you ending your dispute?" Before Evelyn could answer, Artemis continued, "I have been given a small list of required tasks that the fairies expect of me, but please think of other ways that I might be of help to you, and I'll do my best help."

Evelyn thought maybe Artemis was being genuine, and she felt neglectful forgetting that Artemis was behind giving Reed the rock that had helped the siblings make up. "Why, thank you, Artemis, and I'm sorry that I doubted you. I suppose everyone deserves a second chance. I'll try to think of other ways for you to help. In the meantime, feel free to work more with Reed."

"All right, Artemis. Meet me up in my room; I want to talk with Evelyn for a minute, and I'll be up there to get some of my project directions from my backpack," Reed directed Artemis, who vanished in a flash.

"What do you think, sis? I'm pretty convinced that he truly wants to do good. I'm gonna have him help me with my science project, and he can do some of my chores and help with the cleanup work that I'm not a fan of, and . . ." Reed paused to think. "Gosh . . . there's really a whole lot of ways he can help us both!" He smiled broadly as he turned to go to his room.

Artemis waited quietly on Reed's desk by some upright

books as Reed sat in front of him. Reed found his back-pack and pulled out the science project directions. "Hey, Artemis. You know, I don't ever think that I apologized for swatting you when we first crossed paths back in the horse barn. It was sort of an accident, you know. You were buzzing around me so fast, I thought you were a big horse-fly, and I was super annoyed at the noise around my eyes and ears—well, I just couldn't take it anymore."

Artemis wasn't buying Reed's explanation at the moment and only stood and grinned as Reed continued.

"You know, I got so caught up in getting my fort built that I really didn't tune into the doubts I had in the back of my mind, Artemis, and now that Evelyn's brought them up, I wonder . . . Yes, you have done several things to help us, but how do we know it's not just to get all of your magic powers back? How do I know that I can fully trust you?"

Reed felt as if he were being pulled in different directions. He wasn't sure how many ways Artemis would have to prove himself before Reed could fully trust him. He thought back to experiences with friends who'd had trouble keeping the truth and how long it took to regain full trust.

"I'll just have to earn your trust like your sister said, in baby steps. Why not give me another try, Reed?"

Guardedly, Reed accepted his offer. "I have to work on

my science project that's due by the end of the week. Since Evvie is so good at baking, I was planning on getting her help using science in a baking demonstration, but maybe it would help her if I use you instead and leave her alone so she has more time to do her own homework."

Artemis assisted Reed all afternoon, with Reed directing the science steps and Artemis helping with baking ingredients. The project was ready to move to the experimental step the next day, and Reed was enjoying the added help he was getting from Artemis.

After school the next day, Evelyn inquired while cleaning up after their snacks, "How are you coming along on the science project? I'd be happy to share any tips with you if you want."

"Thanks, Evvie, I'll ask if I need anything. Of course, Artemis could bring me just about anything with a wave of his hand, and today, I plan on organizing all the visual aids and then practicing our first run of the experiment. I'll need to use the kitchen to bake several items today and tomorrow."

"What are you going to bake?"

"I plan on using a blueberry muffin recipe four ways—each with a different type of flour, and then recording how sturdy the muffin is based on the flour used. Mrs. Wogen, our science teacher, called it the muffin's 'structure,' so I'm planning on calling the experiment 'How Different Flour Proteins Affect Blueberry Muffin Density.'"

"How is Artemis going to help you?"

"You remember how good he was at cleaning up dishes. He can help, too, with the experiment while I make the muffins."

"Don't take too long with him. He and his pixie friends played a huge trick on me, and I could use help with a recipe that I'm struggling with."

"You? Struggle with a recipe? It must be pretty complex. What are your plans?"

"I want to make a special cake for Mom and Dad's anniversary this weekend, and I'd like to try another new technique, but the recipe I want to use is missing a key ingredient that I'm certain I won't find at the grocery store and I think Artemis could help."

"Did someone call my name?" Artemis floated into the room, returning as he stretched from an afternoon snooze. "It's rather difficult to sleep when people are talking." He quickly recognized his pompous tone and corrected it at once. "What can I do, and for whom? You know, I'm rather proud of myself, as I've been checking things off the list the fairies gave me, and I'm making note of all the ways that I've helped you and your family. Fortunately for me, I've already got a couple of atonement tasks completed."

Curious, Evelyn wondered what the tasks were. "Artemis, may I see the list the fairies gave you?"

Artemis reached into his pants pocket and handed Evelyn the tiny parchment paper listing the ways he had to make atonements to the Gunderson household. After unrolling the itty-bitty scrolled paper, Evelyn grabbed the magnifying glass from the kitchen desk drawer, read it thoroughly, and then read it again. She noticed that each task Artemis was to complete was a result of pixie mischief involving the family:

Atonement Tasks for Pixie Capture #10A.00723

1. Dog
2. Ice
3. Glider
4. Necklace
5. Image
6. Tart
7. Youth

"Oh, I get it, Artemis." Evelyn looked at Reed. "So he has to make up for the tricks he and the pixies played on us when we first moved in."

Artemis further explained, "Each task that I complete–if I complete it successfully–should also help me to acquire a more positive character trait. At least that's what the fairies told me. The Fairy Council believes that once

I've acquired all seven character traits, I'll be free to go on my own . . . and I should have all my magical powers back." While the second part of that statement created much excitement in Artemis, the first part of it scared him. He had no idea what he'd do with himself when he was done serving the fairies.

Looking for more clarification, Evelyn probed, "If I understand this list, you have to use the glider and necklace as part of your atonement, and you've already made improvements to those items, right?" She looked up at Reed. "Yeah, now that that I think of it, we did notice improvements. Remember?"

Before Reed could answer, Artemis interjected, "Ahhh, I'm glad that you noticed the little things that can make your world better." A glimpse of Artemis's old character began to seep into the conversation. "But appreciate it, because I only helped you with those items because the Fairy Council told me that I had to."

Evelyn chose to ignore the comment. "According to this list, you can check *necklace* and *glider* off your list. We didn't think they needed improvements, but now that they've been made better, we'll enjoy them even more! Thanks."

Reed added, "And you can check *dog* off the list because Artemis gave Rupert treats and played a long time with him. That's one thing that Rupert can never get enough of–playtime. He loved the attention, and I think he actually likes you now."

"You're catching on to how the Fairy Council's list works." Artemis was pleased with the start he'd made accomplishing the tasks.

"Why didn't the fairies include the huge catastrophe of glitter that was scattered all over Reed as one of the crimes to be make, uh, what did the fairies call it? Oh yeah, atonements. Well, that glitter stuff was a huge problem that I really think you and the pixies need to atone for. I'm sure Reed and I won't soon forget the job of cleaning that up."

"What glitter are you talking about? Pixies don't have access to glitter. Only fairies do. It sounds like you went through the Gauntlet of Glitter," Artemis said matter-of-factly.

"The Gauntlet of Glitter?" Evelyn repeated. "How can you not remember dumping glitter all over Reed and Rupert after they entered the pine woods? It happened just after we moved into our home." Evelyn was indignant as she looked at Reed.

"Yeah, that's an episode I won't soon forget. It took a lot of work to remove all that glitter."

Artemis explained how the pixies experienced the

same treatment whenever they approached the pine forest closely, which is why the pixies mostly avoided it.

"You can't believe how much it drains the pixies' powers trying to remove the glitter from sticking all over us, and don't think that you can believe everything you hear from the fairies. They want you to think they're all about beauty, loving the earth, and peacefulness. Ha!"

Evelyn and Reed looked at each other, not knowing whom or what to fully believe.

"Here's your list back, Artemis. I need to really get back to today's homework," Evelyn said.

She and Reed put the new information about the fairies in the backs of their minds.

Returning to work on the science project, Artemis recorded the baking results that Reed dictated to him and then Artemis set about cleaning the dishes with a wave of his hands. It was Artemis's hope that with every task completed on his list, more of his magic would return. As the two worked for a few days on Reed's experiment, Artemis found he was really enjoying himself, and he particularly liked Reed's requests for help; he felt needed in a good way. He also liked that Reed seemed to enjoy his help, but he began to worry about losing his pixie touch, which he had worked years to craft. Although a solid friendship with Reed grew, Artemis mumbled under his breath, "I won't lose all my pixie ways if it's the death of me."

As another batch of muffins came out of the oven, Reed felt it was a good time to learn more about the real Artemis. "Do you miss being with your pixie friends?"

"Yes, I really do, but I try not to think about it. It was a lot of fun being a pixie, and we had so many great laughs together." Artemis tried not to smile as he thought back on some of his past pranks.

"Why did you like making life difficult for others?" Reed asked, scooping batter into muffin tins.

"We don't even think about that when we play fun pranks; we're just having a good time in the moment. Then we'd talk about the trick with each other, and it was as if we were reliving it all over again." Artemis looked up in thought. "Yep, those were the good ol' days."

"So you really think that making people feel bad is fun?"

"Of course not. We don't think about that part, just ourselves and the fun we're having." Artemis was perturbed by Reed's questions, so he changed the subject. "What job do you want me to do next?"

They went on to finish the experiment and collect the needed data for the science fair the next day. Wanting to practice his presentation before performing it in front of his parents later that evening, Reed began talking the experiment through in front of the mirror.

"While you practice, it's time for me to check on Evelyn and see how I can help her," Artemis announced as he flew into her room, finding her at her computer. "What are you doing, Evelyn?"

"I'm trying to find out more about a special cake called a gâteau. It's one I've never made before, and I'd really like to surprise my parents by baking it for their anniversary."

"What can I do? I'm finished helping Reed for now."

"Hmm. Do you know anything about a gâteau?"

"I don't know much about cakes of any kind, and a lot less about that kind of cake." Artemis continued as he read over the recipe, "but I do know where to get some ambrosia. I notice that's an ingredient you need for your recipe, and typically, the fairies can get you loads of it–that is, when it's in season. By now, their ambrosia supply has been depleted, and they're just beginning the planting stage for next year's ambrosia crop." Artemis leaned in to Evelyn as if to share a secret. "I can bring you some of a pixie bootleg version that tastes like the real thing, and it shouldn't jeopardize my repentance for the fairies, although I'll need to get their permission to enter enemy territory first."

"Oh no! I certainly wouldn't want you to get in trouble because you were helping me out." Evelyn thought a little more. "But if you could get some ambrosia, I'd love to use it in my cake." She felt torn between getting the rare ingredient and possibly jeopardizing Artemis's atonement goals, much less his life. Being able to use an ingredient she had never baked with before, one that was seldom seen in grocery stores, was an exceptional opportunity, and Artemis assured her that he would not take any unnecessary risks. "Artemis, if you get some ambrosia, I'd be very grateful, but I still can't help but feel that you might get in trouble for my sake."

"The risk is not as big as you think just as long as the fairies are aware of what I'm willing to do for you and they return to me some of the magic I might need to use. I'll be back as soon as possible. While I can't make any promises, I'll do my best. Just know that I have to go back to pixie territory, and they won't give it up willingly. I'm off first to get the fairies' permission." Artemis was proud of himself for even thinking to offer help. The old Artemis wouldn't help anyone, and he would never put himself in danger to do it. "One more thing–if I'm not back by tomorrow, then you'd best be thinking of other ingredients to use in your cake instead."

"Thank you, Artemis. I greatly appreciate your help." Evelyn could see that Artemis was turning over a new leaf.

* * *

It didn't take Artemis long to seek the Fairy Council's permission and explain to them why he was making plans to obtain the bootleg ambrosia from the pixies. They weren't altogether accepting of using this version, but they allowed him to obtain the ingredient this one time and to use a special set of magical powers that would help him instantly disappear if needed.

Artemis next returned to the nearby horse farm, where he and many other pixies resided in the minuscule hidden compartments that provided homes. He remained undercover as he flittered behind a door, then up near a light fixture in the barn, then onto the mane of one of the grazing horses. Not wanting to use magical powers to disappear until he was desperate, he made it through the barn altogether and aimed to approach the area of land just before the river where the water nymphs lived. He knew that he would inevitably cross paths with another pixie who would be aware that the fairies had captured him, so he dirtied himself up a bit more and rehearsed various excuses to explain why he was in the area. He didn't want to jeopardize the work he'd done completing the atonements thus far, and he knew the fairies had sources scattered everywhere who would report any misdeed on his part.

When he reached the land in between the horse farm and the river, just on the edge of pixie territory, he found a small, gated area where the pixie ambrosia was stored. Being familiar with the process they used to make and store the ambrosia, he slipped past the assorted sprites used to guard outdoor pixie property. Sprites were not loyal to either pixies or fairies, but worked for whomever paid the most. After the sprites, he'd have to contend with the pixies who were indoors. Artemis hid using the magical powers allowed by the Fairy Council, but the magic was temporary, causing him to reappear after he'd created a container to carry the siphoned ambrosia. When he was almost through collecting what was needed, he reappeared in the sight line of one of the pixies working on the premises.

"Well, if it isn't my old bestie, Artemis! How are you doing, ol' pal?"

Artemis had never imagined encountering one of his best pixie friends. "Oh, uh, hello, Faerlun. Fancy running into you!" He tried not to stutter as he quickly considered a believable reason for why he was in the area. He found it peculiar that Faerlun did not seem aware of Artemis's capture, as Artemis felt sure he was pictured on the pixies' "WANTED" list. "How are you? Gosh, it's been so long since we last spoke–and hehe, played a trick or two, right?"

Faerlun put his hand to his mouth, as if to cover his chuckling in recalling the fun they'd had pulling pranks. Artemis, meanwhile, tried hard to appear as if everything was as normal as could be. He let out a slight laugh

"What brings you around to our facility?"

Because Faerlun didn't mention the capture, Artemis carried on as if nothing were out of the ordinary. Artemis summoned all the confidence he could and calmly stated, "I've gotten a recent placement as pixie assessor, and I've been assigned to review these premises as well as ensure that the procedures are properly being carried out to produce our version of ambrosia." He was pleased and a little surprised at his deftness in coming up with the excuse under pressure.

"Why, of course! Well, Artemis, I'd like to stay and talk, but I have a meeting with some pixie dignitaries who will be surprised to hear that I ran into you!" Faerlun turned quickly to leave before Artemis had a chance to respond.

Hugely relieved that he had not blown his cover, Artemis moved to act fast, before word got out that he was there. He knew anything that had fairy influence was despised by the pixies. He gathered more than enough of the bootleg ambrosia for Evelyn's cake and used his temporary magical powers to disappear, which proved necessary as he quietly made his way past guards. Fortunately, he was able to return without incident to the kitchen, where Reed was studying and Evelyn was busy working on her gâteau. She had already baked and cooled the cakes, and he was returning just in time for her to prepare the ambrosia filling.

To avoid startling Evelyn, he set the ambrosia container on the counter just loud enough to gain her attention. He darted out from behind the container, which was heavy for him to carry but still just manageable. She turned toward the sound and stopped when she noticed Artemis on the kitchen counter. "Oh, hello, Artemis. Am I glad to see you!"

"Here's your star ingredient. You see, you were able to count on me and my help! But believe me, it wasn't easy; I almost got caught."

"Oh no. Are you all right? I'm glad you made it safely back." She took the ambrosia and set it down next to the work area in the kitchen. What kind of trouble did you encounter?"

"Well, let's just say that I risked my life to get an ingredient for you."

Because of Artemis's past, Evelyn wasn't sure how much truth was behind his statement. "Thank you very much, Artemis, especially since you risked your life." She held up the container of ambrosia to view it in the light and then slipped off the cover to smell it. "Mmmm, it smells lovely, but before I get to work on my cakes, I've got something important to talk with you about." Her voice was urgent, and all her pleasantness dropped. "While you were gone, Natturia and Sampion were here. They said they knew you had been working hard to make amends to our family, so they wanted to warn you. They really want to see you victorious and eventually make it out of fairy captivity."

Artemis sat down near the ambrosia on the kitchen counter. "That's why I've been working so hard. I want to make it out as quickly as I can, too, but why all the concern?"

"Well, the fairies came to tell us that there's a rogue fairy in their midst. Her name is Narcena, and she wants desperately to sabotage your work on the atonements."

Reed, who had been reviewing his notes on his science experiment, added, "They also think that Narcena may try to hurt you, Artemis."

Artemis looked quizzically at Evelyn and Reed. "Why would Narcena want anything to do with me?"

"I asked the same thing," Reed replied. "I thought all fairies worked to make the earth a better place and wouldn't do anything to harm others.

"Narcena evidently had something bad happen to her when she was young, and since then, she has allowed evil to influence her decisions," Evelyn continued.

"Oh, my," Reed and Artemis muttered in unison. The lone pixie had no idea what to do about this new problem.

Evelyn continued, "When Narcena heard that a pixie had been caught and was making amends, she got very angry that any attention was being spent on a pixie because to her, you're always causing problems. She also said that pixies were perpetual bothers and that the fairies were wasting their time helping you, Artemis." Evelyn continued, even as the expression of concern on Artemis's face deepened. "Sampion also explained Narcena didn't feel that a pixie would desire, or even have the ability, to change for the better."

Artemis would be the first to admit that pixies were, indeed, a troublesome bunch of no-good-doers. Pixies lived for those moments and didn't give a second thought about the future. They couldn't care less what others thought of them, but Artemis had noticed changes in his thinking. He liked that Evelyn and Reed cared to include him in their projects, and it felt good that the kids appreciated his efforts, no matter his size or appearance.

He demanded, "Did you tell the fairies that I am living proof Narcena is wrong? I have been working very hard to turn my pixie ways around. Although I'm not completely sure why, I've been proud of my progress." He stood a little taller as he spoke, and he was not going to let a rogue fairy interfere with the hard work he had done already. He also didn't like the fact that a fairy had judged him without even getting to know him. While his desire to help the pixies had diminished considerably, something inside him had changed. Had the fairies done something to affect his brain? Why did he really care so much what a rogue fairy was going to do? The old Artemis likely would have joined Narcena in her plans to destroy.

"How am I supposed to stop her?" Artemis knew he was no match for a fairy and felt more alone than ever. He was just getting to know Evelyn and Reed, and any former pixie friends were now history. "What am I to do?" Frightened, he looked up at Evelyn and Reed helplessly.

Evelyn and Reed turned to each other, puzzled at how to remedy the situation.

"We'll do our best to help you, Artemis. Let's think about our options while we get this cake finished." Evelyn hoped to distract Artemis from feeling hopeless by turning his attention elsewhere. "We'll have to be on guard in case Narcena shows up."

"I'm outta here. I do my best thinking when I'm just laying on my bed and tossing my glider," Reed announced. "I'll try to come up with ideas to help Artemis, though I have no idea how we're a match for a rogue fairy."

Evelyn was anxious to check out this new ingredient Artemis had brought. "What can you tell me about the ambrosia? I'd guess it's a sweet type of pastry filling, but I have no other information about it."

"This will make your cake taste truly remarkable, but know that just a little goes a long way. I brought you more than you asked for, and I don't think that you need all of it. Remember, this is the bootleg version."

Evelyn was starting to wonder if it was the best idea to bake with an ingredient that she'd never used before, one so foreign and potent. "What do you mean?" she asked.

"I mean that the pixies' version of ambrosia is made up of most of the same ingredients as fairies', but we usually make a couple of small substitutions. There's only a minor taste difference." Artemis tried to be assuring.

"Is it safe for me to eat?"

"I wouldn't offer it to you if it wasn't. I went to a lot of work and risked much to get this special ingredient for your cake."

"I suppose you're right." Evelyn wanted to trust Artemis. With only a moment of contemplation, she decided to give him the benefit of the doubt. "I saved a little batter to make a test cupcake so I could see how the cake would taste with the ambrosia before my parents ate the one I made for them." She took an offset spatula to spread the ambrosia into a hole that she'd made in the center of the cupcake, then she topped it off with frosting and took a bite. "Mmmmmmmmmm. That's heavenly. My parents are going to love this gâteau once I've finished it. Thank you, Artemis. I really appreciate your help in getting the ambrosia and all the trouble that you went through for it. I guess you'll be able to check another item off the list that the Fairy Council gave you."

"Oh, I almost forgot . . ." Artemis pulled out his list and glanced at it. "Thank you for trusting me, Evelyn."

Artemis could hardly believe he was actually thanking someone, but he found that he enjoyed having Evelyn place her trust in him. He had never put much thought into the concept of trust before.

"I need to check on Reed and his science project, so I'll leave you for now," he stated. "When will you give your parents the cake you've made them?"

"Their anniversary is Saturday, so in just a couple of days. I'll leave the cake and other ingredients in the fridge and assemble it on Saturday."

Reed was rehearsing his science presentation in front of the mirror with all the muffins arranged in order from the one with the most structure to the least. The project's labels were in place, and the report was fully typed along with step-by-step explanations. *All that's left is the present-ing and the grading, and I'm sure I'll get an A.*

Artemis entered Reed's room. He found a spot to hide behind a picture frame and listened. He clapped enthusi-astically after hearing Reed's presentation. "Nicely done, Reed. I would expect a very good project grade, indeed! You even taught me a few things! Now what else do you need me to help you with?"

"I just need to pack everything so it's ready to bring to school tomorrow. Otherwise, I'm all set. Thanks for your help. You know, it was fun to bake with you, and you were a big help with kitchen cleanup."

"No problem." As Artemis flew away, he shouted back to Reed, "I'm sure you and your sister will be pleased with the results of your projects and the responses they get! They're going to be big! See you later!"

Ambrosia Gateau

Ambrosia

¾ cups   milk
¾ cups   whipping cream
4   egg yolks
½   cup white sugar
2 cups   flour

To make the ambrosia, heat milk and whipping cream over low heat in a saucepan. In another bowl, stir together egg yolks, sugar, and flour until combined. Increase heat with milk mixture while stirring and ladle one spoonful into egg mixture, making sure not to curdle eggs. Temper egg mixture by adding it back into heated milk mixture, being careful to stir continuously. As mixture heats, it will thicken when it reaches a low boil. Remove and pour into glass bowl. Cover with plastic film, making sure no air is between top of ambrosia and plastic film. Refrigerate until completely cool.

Cake

2½ cups   cake flour
1 tablespoon   baking powder
1 cup   white sugar
¼ teaspoons   kosher salt
2   egg yolks, room temperature
3   eggs, room temperature
½ cup   milk, room temperature
1 cup   vegetable oil
1 tablespoon   vanilla
¾ cups   blackberry jam
  powdered sugar

Preheat oven and prepare cake pan by greasing a 9-inch springform pan. Sift flour together with baking powder. Mix with sugar and salt, and set aside. In another bowl, whisk egg yolks, eggs, oil, vanilla, and milk until pale and creamy. Pour wet mixture into dry ingredients until just combined. Overmixing will cause cake to be dry and less tender.

Pour half of cake batter into the prepared pan. Dollop ambrosia onto cake batter and alternate with small spoonfuls of the blackberry jam. Repeat two more times with batter, jam, and ambrosia in another layer until all are used up. Bake for 30-35 minutes until inserted toothpick comes out clean. Cool on wire rack. Dust with powdered sugar.

11.

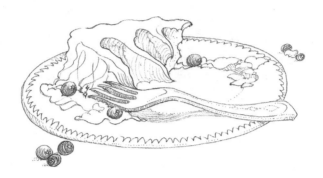

The Rogue Revenge

On the school bus the next day, Reed rested his backpack on the seat next to him. With the boxed science muffins and project materials on his lap, his mind replayed the last conversation that he'd had with Artemis. *What exactly did Artemis mean by saying we'll be pleased with the results of our projects, and the response will be big?* Reed wanted to fully trust Artemis, but there was always a nagging feeling that a joke was about to be pulled or some trick played at his expense. He knew it was just the nature of pixies, pure and simple, and Reed could tell that Evelyn shared a measure of his mistrust. *What does it take for someone to completely change their opinion about something or someone, and how long will it be before it happens?* Reed wondered.

Several classrooms were busy setting up the school-wide science fair with tables displaying projects in each grade level. Reed neatly set up his station with the scientific explanation of his experiment, the hypothesis, the conclusion, etc. The next task was to order the muffins according to the accompanying description and result. When he pulled the last two muffins out of the shoebox he'd used to carry them in, his heart sank, and his stomach began to churn. An enormous bite had been taken out of each. He knew full well that he couldn't use the muffins as part of his display. He began to list and then eliminate possible offenders in his head.

"I'll bet Artemis had something to do with this," he muttered. Now his only recourse was to speak to his teacher about how to best resolve the issue. It was easiest to blame the missing muffin portions on poor Rupert, but Reed knew that the muffins had been well out of Rupert's reach, and he trusted Evelyn, knowing she wasn't capable of this kind of behavior. Fortunately for Reed, his teacher was familiar with his usual conscientious character; he'd give him a second chance to make more muffins for Monday. It was hugely disappointing, however, as the science fair would be over by then, and it wouldn't be nearly as much fun as participating with his friends.

After school, all he could do was let off steam. Evelyn listened intently to him describe the disastrous episode as they sat eating their snacks in the kitchen.

"I knew that I couldn't trust Artemis! What a fool he made of me! I pulled out the last two muffins from the box, and they each had a gigantic bite taken out of them. There was no way I could use them, so I had to pack the whole thing up and watch my friends have fun participating in the science fair. Just wait until I see him. I want to squish him like a bug!"

He waved his arms dramatically as he angrily stumbled over his words. Evelyn could hardly think of how to comfort him. On the one hand, she could certainly empathize with him, and his anger appeared justified, but she couldn't stop wondering why Artemis would play such a mean trick on Reed when he seemed to genuinely have fun helping him and had mentioned he didn't want to give up the magical powers he'd reacquired.

"Do you think that a different pixie could have eaten part of your muffins and maybe it wasn't Artemis who tricked you?"

"I thought of that, but we should still report this to Natturia and Sampion as soon we can and make them aware of what happened. Now I have to spend the weekend baking muffins all over again for Monday."

"I wish I could help, but I have all sorts of homework myself, and Mom and Dad's anniversary cake has to be decorated and assembled. We're celebrating Saturday, but I'll see what I can do to help."

"I'll be up in my room. I just need to think this through." Reed's disappointment in Artemis weighed heavily on his heart, and he couldn't get excited about his science project. "If you happen to see him, don't send him my way. I'm afraid I might do something to him that I'll regret."

"That's horrible!" Evelyn said aloud to Rupert as he sniffed around the kitchen floor for crumbs. "You know, Rupert, I can't help but agree with what the famous psychologist Abraham Maslow said."

"What did Maslow say?" Mrs. Gunderson asked, entering the kitchen with her arms around two large bags of groceries after work.

"Oh, hi, Mom. I was just sharing with Rupert a quote by Maslow that I read once. It said, 'In any given moment, we have two options: to step forward into growth or step back into safety.' Reed just went to his room. It seems there was a big mishap with the muffins he was going to use in his science project, but fortunately for him, his teacher is allowing him to fix it for a Monday presentation."

"Oh, boy, that's not good. What happened? Do you think I ought to see how he's doing?"

"I think he'll be fine once he has a little time to reflect and cool off, and I'll let him tell you about it when he's ready. How was your day?"

"Great! It was one of those days where everything goes according to plan. I want to get a couple of things done around the house since Dad and I'll be going out to dinner for our anniversary tomorrow night. By the way, I agree with Maslow."

Evelyn placed her hand on a recipe to save the spot where she'd left off reading and announced, "You'll have to leave room for a treat after your anniversary dinner. I made a special dessert for when you and Dad get home in honor of your special day. It's in the refrigerator, but you'll have to wait until tomorrow night for the surprise. I came across a new ingredient to try, and I think you'll be impressed."

"Why, Evelyn! How thoughtful of you!" Mrs. Gunderson opened the door to the fridge to take note of the cake. "I'll make sure to let Dad know about your sweet offer, and we'll definitely save room for anything you serve us; your treats are always delectable," she said closing the door.

Evelyn smiled as she always did when her mother bolstered her confidence.

By Saturday evening, an anniversary card was ready to present and the gâteau containing the ambrosia was assembled and served to the entire family. The unique flavor of the ambrosia was well noted, making a fabulously flavored dessert that the family devoured, but the next morning was far from enjoyable, as every member of the Gunderson family had become fantastically groggy while eating, to the point of falling asleep right at the dinner table!

The kitchen was a spectacle with each family member's face planted *on* their desserts, forks still gripped in their hands, and napkins unfolded on their laps. Sounds of breathing, snorting, and snoring echoed through the air. Alongside pools of ambrosia and whipped cream on the table, bits of cake dotted their faces as they started to wake. Further morsels were strewn about their laps, with still other remnants that had missed their intended targets on the floor.

It was midday Sunday when the family began to fully wake up as Rupert jumped on the sides of their chairs, trying to get their attention by licking their dangling hands and tugging at their shoes. Moans and groans came out as each slowly woke, stretching from the positions they had taken for hours at the dining room table. Still groggy and rubbing their eyes to adjust to the daylight, each person became less befuddled looking around the mess they had made the night before.

"Mom?" Evelyn asked as she wiped off pieces of the anniversary dessert still stuck to her cheek. "What happened?"

Reed began to raise his head, watching his dad use a napkin to wipe bits of the gâteau off his face.

"I'm not so sure. The last thing I remember, we were talking and having giggling fits while we were enjoying the dessert you made, Ev. I'm not even sure what time it is now."

Mr. Gunderson looked at the wall clock, brushing crumbs off his blue button-down shirt as he stood up. "What time is it? 12:45? *What?* Did we sleep straight through the night and half the day?" Before anyone could muster a response, he continued, "We must've been up extremely late or we were extremely tired because we didn't even make it to bed, and we completely missed church this morning." His eyes looked around his plate, then to the floor, and then to the window to see the sun high in the sky. "We've never overslept like this before!"

Mrs. Gunderson instantly agreed. "It's so bizarre. I wonder what would've made us sleep in so late; I don't recall being overly tired yesterday. And darling, you're mistaken about how late we were up last night. I specifically recall seeing the clock read 7:00 before feeling very sleepy. I remember laughing so hard, and then I noticed that my legs felt so heavy, all I wanted to do was rest my head on the table. I didn't realize I had rolled my face over to my plate! Anyway, I know your head fell before mine did. I couldn't help laughing uncontrollably at that sight, but for the life of me, I can't think now what was so funny."

"My whole body feels tired," announced Evelyn before quickly rushing off to the bathroom. It wasn't long before the whole family went from feeling exhausted to ill.

Mr. and Mrs. Gunderson did their best to make occasional trips between the bedrooms to check on Evelyn and Reed; they felt they had to use all their energy to look after their children. Fortunately, the illness was short-lived, and when evening rolled around, everyone seemed to be on the road to recovery. It was time to reflect on what had made all four family members so sick.

"Mom, I've hardly been able to keep anything down," Evelyn moaned as she came to the kitchen later. She was partially hunched over, holding her stomach, her face a faint shade of green.

"Well," Reed said as he began giggling and pointing to Evelyn, "you're gonna lift your hand up to remove the cake still attached to your forehead."

Evelyn was not at all amused. The family proceeded to

clean the table, dishes, and floor while thinking about the unusual occurrence.

"Honey, how do you think it was that we became so sleepy and not one of us could excuse ourselves from the table and put ourselves to bed? That just doesn't make any sense," said Mrs. Gunderson.

"I agree, and I'm not sure how to explain any of it," replied her husband. "To think that we sat at the table as we do every day, and then ate dessert to the point of collapsing on our plates . . . It's extraordinary, almost as if we were all put under a spell or something."

"Do you suppose it was something that we ate?"

"We all seemed fine after dinner." Mr. Gunderson looked out the window in thought. "I remember eating nearly all of the dessert that Evelyn made when my head suddenly felt too heavy to hold up."

"That's how I felt, too," Evelyn added. "I remember my arms felt like lead. I could barely hold my fork, but for some reason, I found that feeling hilarious."

Mrs. Gunderson stopped as a possible explanation entered her head. "You don't suppose it was carbon monoxide."

"No, it couldn't have been," Mr. Gunderson said matter-of-factly. "I happened to check on the detectors last week. If it were carbon monoxide, the sensors in the house would have gone off. We wouldn't have slept through that! At any rate, we're fine now, and there doesn't seem to be any harm done."

Evelyn and Reed kept exchanging glances. Each searched the evening's events for clues, but fearing eaves-dropping ears, they headed to their rooms silently to get changed into clean clothes.

Reed knocked on Evelyn's door and peeked in when she acknowledged him. "Hey, Evelyn. Are you thinking what I'm thinking?"

"Hmm, maybe. What are you thinking?"

"I think that your dessert is what made us sleepy and put us down for the count."

Evelyn couldn't help but feel responsible and a little defensive at the same time. It did occur to her because she and Reed had not eaten dinner at the restaurant with their parents, and they *had* eaten the dessert she made . . . well, it was simply hard not to see it add up to this unfortunate question: Could it have been the ambrosia that she had never used before? As she asked herself, she couldn't help but jump to the assumption that Artemis may have been up to his old tricks. She was horribly conflicted while also feeling that she was regaining her full sense of alertness. "Do you think that Artemis could be back to his old ways?"

"I'm not sure what to think anymore! Look, first my

muffins. Now, your dessert. What else are we supposed to think? I'd bet that you would be fuming mad, too." Reed hesitated before going on. "I just don't get it, though. Don't you remember what Artemis told us he went through with those bugs and birds in the oak tree? Losing his magical powers? So then why would he throw that progress away and risk not getting his full powers back?"

"Yeah, I'm not sure what to think either." Evelyn gathered up her soiled clothes and towels to throw in her laundry basket, but her heart was very heavy. She could hardly bear to think that something she'd made for her family to enjoy had caused a large mess in more ways than one.

She brought her laundry downstairs, where she ran into her mom again. "I still question, Mom, if it was the ambrosia that made us sleepy because I ate some of it in a cupcake the day before, and I felt completely fine after eating it."

"It has to be the ambrosia," her mother surmised as she separated the dirty laundry. "We just can't think of anything else it could have been. Where did you find ambrosia to use anyway?"

Evelyn could only think to tell her that she got the ambrosia from a specialty store online, and then she went back to Reed's room.

"Reed, wasn't Artemis going to stop by before the

weekend was over to see how our projects went?"

"If he does, I really don't want to talk to him—not for a very long time."

"Maybe we should talk to Natturia and Sampion first. They'll want to know about what happened with the science experiment and my dessert. I thought long and hard, and I believe Artemis is back to his pixie ways now that he can use some of his magical powers."

Reed stated sternly, "No matter how many times a snake sheds its skin, it's still a snake. Don't you agree?"

"I do. Let's summon the fairies before we run into Artemis."

The two joined hands, closed their eyes, and wished with all their might to speak to the fairies, who appeared just moments later behind Reed's head. Once the fluorescent glow subsided, Natturia and Sampion became visible, holding hands and floating down to stand on Reed's desk.

Looking up to the children and filled with much optimism, Natturia was the first to speak.

"Greetings. It is a glorious day, don't you think?" But before any answer could be uttered, she became aware of the children's expressions. "What's new? You don't look particularly well."

Evelyn addressed both fairies as Reed looked on. "We have another problem."

"With Narcena?" Sampion asked.

Reed shot back, "No, with Artemis. It looks like he's back to his old ways."

"What happened?" Disappointment filled Natturia's face. "He was making such great progress, and it seemed that he would even gain some of the privileges that we fairies possess."

Once the weekend's unfortunate episodes were relayed to them, Natturia and Sampion returned to the Fairy Council to discuss the terms of Artemis's reparations. It looked as if Artemis was now in danger of not only losing all his magical powers again, but being assigned to the PSI–Perpetual Sealand of Indemnity, a place designated for offenders to make up for their crimes indefinitely.

Natturia and Sampion returned to inform Reed and Evelyn of this news and instructed them to be on the lookout for Artemis before disappearing once again.

* * *

Reed was trying to focus on homework at his bedroom desk, but Evelyn couldn't stop thinking about what might happen to Artemis. She stopped by his room to pick up laundry and asked, "Why do you think he would trick us if he knew he might end up at this Perpetual

Sealand place?"

Before Reed could answer, Artemis floated to the windowsill and asked, "Why are you talking about the Perpetual Sealand?"

"How long have you been standing there?" Evelyn inquired. She'd save her anger and pour it out in full force when the time was right—even though she wasn't usually the type to get very mad.

Artemis was his usual cheery self as he stood on Reed's desk, looking innocent enough.

"Evelyn and I would love to have your head on a platter right now, Artemis. How can you stand there so innocently when you know perfectly well that you ruined our family's weekend in every possible way?" Reed couldn't help the tears that fell down his cheeks, feeling so betrayed after investing so much time in his science project and in getting close to Artemis.

Evelyn put her arm around Reed to comfort him, her face stern. "How could you be so rotten, Artemis? We trusted you to be our friend and help us with the projects we were working on, but you just couldn't help yourself, could you? I suppose you just felt compelled to pull a few more pranks."

Artemis stood with his mouth open wide, completely

bewildered. He had absolutely no idea what had happened in the Gunderson household that weekend, but he could see how completely distraught Evelyn and Reed were. "Guys, what happened?" It was hard to defend himself, he thought, if he didn't even know what crimes he had supposedly committed.

Reed scowled. "How did my muffins taste? I hope they were worth ruining all my work!" He threw himself on the bed and stuffed his face into a pillow to quiet his extreme irritation.

Evelyn grimaced as she folded her arms with authority. "Let me ask you—did you taste any of the ambrosia you gave me? I wonder if you would've gotten sick like we did. No one in our family thought feeling ill because we ate the ambrosia was the least bit funny."

"Guys, I'm very sorry those things happened to you, but I swear to you on my life"—he enunciated each word for emphasis—"I had nothing to do with either of those events. Remember all the work I've done to help you; why would I want to risk hurting our friendship or losing my magical powers after I had just regained them? You know how important that was to me. And why in the world would I risk getting caught by the pixies, only to watch your family get sick? That wouldn't make any sense."

Did he have a *real* friendship with the kids? Had the friendship become important to him? With tears welling in his eyes and then spilling down his cheeks, Artemis realized another first; he truly felt bad for Evelyn and Reed and wished he could take away their pain and sadness.

The children looked at each other, a little puzzled, not knowing what to believe.

"I guess that does make some sense," Evelyn muttered. "But then who would you say took those large bites out of Reed's muffins? And what's your explanation for why the ambrosia made my entire family so tired and ill?"

"Listen, I've had my guard up ever since news of Narcena arrived, and my eyes and ears have been wide open just in case she strikes. Have you seen her or any sign that she's been around?"

Evelyn and Reed looked at each other and sat a little straighter. "I forgot all about the threat of Narcena."

"Yeah, I was so angry about my science project that I didn't even think about her."

"If it wasn't you who damaged our projects, Artemis, we're sorry. Understand that when someone acts a certain way over and over again, people sometimes come to expect more of the same." Evelyn found herself sounding a little like her parents again.

"Is that why you were speaking about the P-p-perpetual Sealand of Indemnity?" Artemis asked fearfully. He and all the other pixies were well aware of what the PSI was; they had enjoyed teasing each other about the possibility of being caught. "Surely, I've done nothing to be considered for that evil place!"

"We just told Natturia and Sampion we thought you were the instigator of our recent problems, but now that you've brought up Narcena, we'd better let them know right away that she may be the one causing the problems. We don't want to see you get blamed for something she did, if that really is the case." Doubts about Artemis still lingered in Evelyn's mind, but the more she reflected on the explanation he'd given for why he hadn't committed the recent crimes, the clearer it became that it was, indeed, Narcena who'd sabotaged them. She certainly had a motive.

"Won't you believe me? I . . . I really like you, and I've actually had fun working with you on your projects. It's made me forget my worries about where I'll be after I'm finished with the atonement tasks," Artemis pleaded, tears welling up in his eyes. He knew there was the added threat that he may not carry out all the remaining tasks with Narcena in the midst. He decided not to worry about her for now and simply move forward; he had been feeling stronger with each completed task, and he found the more he worried, the less focus he had on the work at hand and the less creative and resourceful he was.

He had turned a corner regarding his appearance as well. He now walked with more confidence; he held his head higher, he had been smiling more lately, and his wings turned from the usual gray color to a pale, softer, bluish pastel. Yes, it appeared he no longer looked like a curmudgeonly, mischief-making pixie.

Evelyn couldn't help but think that the kindness Artemis recently displayed was softening his old image. His gnarly grin had become a genuinely soft smile, and he looked altogether more approachable. It was easy to note that his posture had improved as he stood more upright with the recently acquired self-confidence.

"We'll explain what's happened to the fairies, Artemis, why we really think that it was Narcena who sabotaged us and how you actually helped us," she said.

Reed stood and addressed Artemis. "I'm sure we can convince them that it was Narcena and not you who bit my muffins and made us sick eating the gâteau." He would be able to return to the kitchen to make more muffins, now that he no longer felt betrayed by Artemis.

"If it was Narcena who sabotaged us, then I'd consider you successful in helping Reed and me with our projects," Evelyn suggested.

Artemis smiled as he felt his relationship with Evelyn and Reed return to friendlier terms. "I'll work on another task while you get the word from the fairies that I'm cleared to continue, and maybe they'll find a way to restrain Narcena if she's going to harm others."

"Artemis! Do you realize what you just said?" Evelyn's voice was excited as she stood up from the desk chair. "You said that you didn't want Narcena to hurt others, which means you care that she's not successful with her bad choices. You know, I think that you wear integrity well!" Evelyn smiled enthusiastically.

Artemis thought for a minute. He couldn't argue that he didn't want Narcena to hurt others, much less himself, and because he had long practiced performing misdeeds and tricks on others, he'd never taken the time to consider an alternative. He just thought that mischief-making was what made a pixie a true pixie.

"Come to think of it, Evelyn, I do care, not only about what Narcena does to me but I also care very much about what she does to others. Well, what do you know? I am a pixie who cares." Artemis paused, looking serious again. "What's happening to me? Do you think this disqualifies me from being a pixie?" He was not totally convinced that he had changed for the better, because the ways he showed he cared seemed too small to be considered real change. "I couldn't go back to the pixie clan even if I wanted to, so maybe integrity is something that will stay with me."

"Not necessarily." Evelyn sat back in her chair. "After you've completed the atonement tasks, you could go back to your old ways of playing tricks on others, you know."

Reed glanced back at Artemis and gave him a serious look, clearly suggesting that doing so would *not* be a good idea.

Artemis instantly understood Reed's expression as he folded his legs to sit. "I understand; I really don't think the happiness I felt being a pixie is as great as the happiness I feel now. I should also clarify with the Fairy Council which tasks are considered completed, and then I'll know better what to do next. I do feel better after we had this talk. I'm finding that my heart warms whenever I see one of you smile, and when I have another item checked off the list, I feel even better"–Artemis hung his head–"even though I have no idea where I'll be or what I'll do when I'm finished completing the work for the Fairy Council."

Rather than dwell on uncertainty, he decided to work to hold the despair inside; he tried to concentrate on the positive changes occurring within himself. He stood back up. "I'll be back as quickly as I can after I consult with the Fairy Council and report to you what I find out."

Evelyn felt compelled to point out, "Don't forget to tell the Fairy Council that you risked your life to help me with my cake."

"And that you helped me and Evelyn recon . . . recon . . . oh, Evelyn. What's the word that I'm trying to say?" asked Reed.

"I think you're trying to say *reconcile*–and that we did, dear brother," Evelyn answered as she put her arm around Reed, happy that he still looked to her for answers.

"Good thinking, Evelyn and Reed." This time, Artemis was able to wave and disappear among what looked like a flurry of colored dust particles.

As the dust settled, Evelyn put her hand to her chin and inquired, "Reed, don't you think he looks a little different now? I mean, I remember him looking harsher and colder when we first met him. Of course, that was when he was hurt, but beyond that, there was nothing remarkable about him. Remember? He had dull coloring and was lackluster in every other sense–inside and out. I think he's starting to look a little more like one of those fairies. Don't you think his color is changing a little? And he looks happier." Evelyn thumbed absent-mindedly through a notebook on her lap and sighed. She continued, "I sure hope everything goes well at the Fairy Council. If it was Narcena who sabotaged us, then he should surely be allowed to finish the atonement tasks."

Reed agreed. "I'd feel really bad for Artemis if the Fairy Council didn't let him finish."

"I would, too. In fact, I think he's completed most of the tasks. Let's check to see what he has left to do when he comes back."

"You mean *if* he comes back. He might have to stay with the fairies if they believe the rogue fairy over him." Reed glanced at Evelyn as he sat down on the edge of his bed, looking as forlorn as Rupert losing his best and favorite toy.

Several minutes of silence filled the room as the two reflected over Artemis's future prospects. It was broken as Natturia and Sampion returned, fluttering in the air before the children's eyes. "We're so glad to find you both together. After discussing the latest developments with our leaders, you'll be pleasantly surprised . . ." Natturia paused.

Sampion continued, "Just so long as you can understand the reasoning behind the fairies' actions. You'll want to sit down as we tell you more of what we learned about Narcena." The two fairies took their usual spot on the bedroom dresser. "It is our deep hope, when we are finished explaining all we've learned from our leaders, that you will understand what's been done in the name of the greater good for Artemis."

An important discussion commenced as the fairies explained their leader's intentions in detail. Both kids, sitting on the edge of their seats, focused intensely on what the fairies were telling them. After much nodding, Narcena's true purpose became clear to Reed and Evelyn. Their faces filled with obvious enlightenment and the assurance that everything would work out. The very serious conversation ended with Evelyn smiling and Reed announcing, "Oh, now I get it."

The Fairy Forum

Inside the old oak tree, about midway up, Artemis sat in the same courtroom he had before. He was alone at a table, waiting yet again for the arrival of the Fairy Council. In front of where he sat, the three council members entered and reviewed their notes as Artemis steadied his gaze on them. Their faces were always void of emotion, so he had no way of knowing whether he would face good news or not. Making the choice to present whatever positive front he could muster, he felt he had to try his best to follow their directions and fulfill all their tasks, and, for the most part, do it willingly. He desperately wanted to avoid the PSI—an incomparable place of misery.

He put a lot of thought into the steps he had taken and the changes he had experienced, as well as the substantial effort and sacrifice he'd made to help Evelyn obtain the ambrosia. He felt he had plenty of reasons to support why he should be allowed to keep completing the atonement tasks, and he was ready to fight any reason Narcena offered for why he should not be allowed to continue.

Why does Narcena have such a drive to see me fail? Artemis wondered. "Anyone would see that it's just plain unfair; I'd even go as far as to say that she has a prejudice against pixies, or maybe it's just against me," he whispered. He was so focused on the conversation he was having with himself, he hadn't noticed that the council members were ready to begin.

The bailiff announced loudly, "All rise. The court will now come to order. The honorable Fairy Council members will now reside over Fairy Forum session A1025.0046. What say you, Artemis?"

"Um . . . uh, excuse me, Your Honors," Artemis stumbled over his words. "I, um . . . I-I'm sorry. I was deep in thought as I reflected on my recent behavior."

"That's a good place for us to start," the Fairy Council said sternly.

Artemis looked across at the other side of the room, where Narcena was to argue her points.

Why hasn't she shown up yet? Artemis thought. He continued aloud, "I'm here to see if I have your permission to continue the atonement tasks." Looking down at the crumpled list he kept in his pocket, he mentally checked off tasks as he explained to the council how each was completed. "I helped the family dog; in fact, I even became quite friendly toward the animal. I gave the dog a food supply and toys that will create a new-and-improved Rupert, complete with a stunning coat, more energy, and intelligence beyond imagination," he explained to the Fairy Council. "I also enhanced the boy's glider and the girl's necklace, and they seemed very satisfied, Your Honors. Additionally, I helped Reed build and tear down his fort; that wasn't on your original list. Oh, and I also used my magical powers to create a mind-reading stone that helped Evelyn and Reed resolve a conflict, and I did that out of the kindness of my heart." Artemis continued, looking down at his list, "And let me see . . . I helped the children with their projects, which I think would check both *youth* and *tart* off the atonement list, except"–Artemis paused–"there was little a problem that came up." He felt his heart sink to his stomach as he thought back to the heartbreak and anger in Evelyn and Reed's voices after the disasters with their projects.

He was interrupted by one of the council members. "We understand that Narcena, a relatively high-ranking fairy, allegedly sabotaged you and that you wonder if the tasks will be considered successfully completed in spite of what she did. Is that correct?"

"Exactly, Your Honor." Artemis wondered how the Fairy Council already knew about it.

"Why should we consider your word over hers?"

"Because, Your Honor, I've been working hard to complete the tasks. I have tried to complete each of them willingly, to the best of my ability, and in ways that would fully make up for having made life more difficult for others."

"I like your reasoning," one of the Fairy Council leaders commented. "Go on."

Artemis continued with passion, "I went considerably out of my way to get an ingredient for Evelyn, and even risked being captured—or worse—by the pixies."

"So we've noticed, but how do we know you really care for the Gunderson family? After all, you once very much enjoyed playing many tricks on them."

Artemis wanted to be as convincing as possible so that the Fairy Council would see his heart. "Before I completed the atonement tasks, I didn't know how much it would mean to be a help to someone. I saw the joy the Gunderson children had when I fixed the necklace and the glider; it gave me such a warm feeling inside—one that I've never felt before, and it made me truly happy. Sort of like I was getting a gift in return. Even the dog had fun playing with me, and believe me, it's a lot more fun to have a dog lick you than try to take a bite out of you!"

Compelled to make certain the Fairy Council understood the depth of his feelings, he continued, "I also felt emotions that I've never felt before when I finished some of the tasks, Your Honor. For example, I've never before known joy, but when I was helping Evelyn and Reed, my heart was full of this new and incredible feeling, and when Narcena sabotaged their projects, I couldn't stop myself from crying. I wanted to make their pain go away and fix their projects for them. By helping them reach their goals, I saw that I was having fun, and then I noticed that I started feeling closer to them." Artemis gave himself a gentle hug as he described the relationship he had developed with the kids. "I'm not sure how else to say that the friendship I have with them now means a great deal to me. I'd help them in any way I could, and it brings me much happiness and contentment to be around their family. And yes, I get mad now if I think any of the pixies are doing anything against the Gunderson family."

Artemis couldn't finish without bringing up a couple

of important points. "Finally, Your Honor, I'd like to add that I had the opportunity to lash out at Narcena because her actions made us all angry, but I chose not to. Instead, I wanted to set a good example for Evelyn and Reed. Oh, and I went to a lot of trouble just to get a small ingredient for Evelyn; I even made sacrifices . . ." Artemis stopped, realizing he had already made this point and was back to focusing more on himself than others. "Uh . . . sorry. I guess I said that already. It's just that I sort of surprised myself in how I accomplished getting the ambrosia in spite of the obstacles. But the point is how happy Evelyn felt, knowing I helped her."

"One more thing, as I see it. I have successfully completed all the tasks but one, and I hope you will see that although Narcena gave me reason to want to quit, I did not." Artemis looked over at the empty chair and table across the room. "It also looks to me like Narcena didn't care enough to argue her point, because she didn't even show up."

He knew that he probably should have left that point alone and let Narcena's absence speak for itself. He hung his head as he nervously awaited the council's decision when a brightly colored finch signaled that he would have to wait even longer while in a holding cell. As Artemis got up to leave, the sentry squirrel motioned to him that he should pick up his atonement task list left behind on the table. Artemis took a deep breath and retrieved the paper, folding it to store in his pocket. When he picked up the list, he recalled that each task would reveal a positive characteristic once successfully carried out. He was looking forward to viewing the new list.

As the squirrel guard led him to his holding cell, he thought of how the old Artemis wouldn't have cared less if the atonement task list would transform; the truth was that the old Artemis would not have seen a point in improving himself. Normal pixies would simply focus on why they had to complete the atonement tasks in the first place, and they relished holding feelings of resentment, self-pity, and spite. He thought, too, how those dark feelings in the past often created more negative feelings of self-disgust, which had hardened his facial features, making a creature who grew more stone-hearted and unsympathetic. He liked the new-and-improved Artemis, and he felt more openness, a greater sense of peacefulness, and an increased desire to share his happiness with others.

The holding cell was dimly lit, and when the solid, thick door closed tightly behind him, there was only silence. Artemis could hear his heartbeat as he sat looking around his cell. "I wonder what's taking the council members so long to decide whether or not I should be allowed to finish the one task left, or maybe they're taking more time deciding whether they should consider the sabotaged tasks as completed." He looked around at the barren, dark cell. He was resigned to consider a couple of tasks as do-overs if needed. "It's not like I'm anxious to go back to the pixies anymore; I wouldn't like it with them much, anyways–at least not like I used to."

Life with the pixies would never be what he remembered if he returned. He was certain of that much. As he waited in silence, listening to the rhythmic beating of his heart, he could see that he no longer desired what the pixie life offered. He stretched out on the cot and reread the atonement list, reflecting briefly on each task and how it was completed. He scratched a check mark next to each completed task with his long nail. The only item not checked was the fifth one: Image. "I wonder what the fairies mean by *Image*?" Whose image was he supposed to help fix? Was the image outward or inward? What image had been damaged by the pixies? "I wish Evelyn and Reed were here to discuss this with me. They'd give me some answers."

A guard commanded him to open the cell door and to exit into a corridor. At this point, Artemis had had hours to reflect. He followed the guard, walking in silence down the narrow hallway to the courtroom, where he once again found himself alone at a table in front of the Fairy Council.

Looking across at the adjacent table, Artemis found that it remained empty. Minutes turned into an hour of waiting, when the council finally arrived. This time, there was no bailiff present, and the Fairy Council did not wear their usual robes. The center council member spoke first.

"Artemis, we are pleased to tell you that your behavior and atonement tasks have been well received. They are considered completed at this time, and we'll further share with you that Narcena was never an actual threat, as she never existed."

Artemis didn't know what to say or think. "Ummm, I don't understand, Your Honor."

"Narcena was merely our way to test you, Artemis. How you reacted to the ways we sabotaged your work revealed to us whether or not you qualified to join the fairies; since your return to the pixies could never be completed because the fairies have had an influence on you, we wanted to ensure that you have developed a new set of characteristics that will help you move forward. We didn't want to have to negotiate your return to the pixies, anyways."

Stunned, Artemis tried to sort out his feelings about this. *Narcena never existed?* That statement alone made his head swirl. He cleared his throat.

"Did I hear you correctly? You're saying Narcena never existed, and you made her up so you could test me?" He fumed, but he controlled any outward display of anger by biting hard on his tongue and wringing his hands firmly. He could hear air leaving his nose as he expelled for a length of time, and he clenched his teeth. Then he finally took a breath in very slowly, trying to remain positive. He wasn't going to give the council the satisfaction of seeing him get angry.

"With all due respect, if fairies do wonders of beauty and kindness . . . Well, if you fairies are so nice, why did you make Reed so sad and angry at me? Because of what Narcena—I mean, the fairies—did, he had to start his science project all over again. And how come the whole Gunderson family fell into a deep sleep after eating Evelyn's dessert that I know she worked hard on? That doesn't seem fair or very nice of you, and I'm sorry if this seems rude, but it wasn't very nice at all. I think it downright contradicts what you fairies have always said you represent." Artemis took another deep breath and waited for a reaction from the council members, fully expecting them to suggest that his remarks had crossed the line.

The middle council member at the table stood as if to confront Artemis who thought, perhaps, he was not only going to receive a reprimand but an additional punishment. "You are bold, Artemis, but you most certainly have a right to question us. And if you question authority respectfully, we cannot deny that you are deserving of an answer. After all, your success entirely hinges on how you respond to unfortunate events and setbacks. For your information, it was the Duo Supreme Dieties who decided to test you this way, and it remains the fairy creed to do what is right and beautiful in this world. It was the Dieties' expert opinion, after thoroughly conducting research into the hearts of the Gunderson family, that they would understand the tests would help you to convert your behavior fully. We saw that you had potential, and so did the Gundersons. While you were in your holding cell waiting, our methods have been fully explained to the children. Know, too, that there are additional facts you are not aware of at this moment, though in due time, you will find complete understanding. As a side note, however, you presented Evelyn with a bootleg version of ambrosia. Had you used a wholly authentic fairy variety of ambrosia, I believe the Gundersons would not have fallen so deeply asleep. However, we we won't hold that against you as you were trying to serve a good purpose."

The eldest council member leaned forward and looked directly at Artemis, stating enthusiastically, "And you succeeded with flying colors, Artemis! You had the opportunity to take the magical powers we had returned to you and use them against Narcena, but you chose not to. You also chose to persevere when the tasks became difficult. Think back to how difficult it was to get the ambrosia; you worked very hard to help Evelyn."

"Artemis, we cannot tell you how pleased we are at your accomplishments," interjected the third council member. "Only one other previously captured pixie has accomplished as much as you have and without turning back to its previous lifestyle. We are returning all your magical powers, as we are confident you will use them to help others."

Artemis was thrilled, but he also had so many other questions. He suddenly stopped in mid-thought. *What? There are other pixies who have been captured? What happened to them? What did they have to do to win their freedom, if they were freed at all? Were they not successful at mastering their atonement tasks, and where is the other pixie who was successful?* Enough about them; he was so close to being free. Artemis wanted to only focus on himself for now. He was so overjoyed to be finished with his atonement tasks and to have his magical powers returned, he couldn't have been happier. He wanted to dance and sing, but there were still some questions to be answered.

"Your Honor, I don't completely understand. When I look at the atonement list, it still shows that I have one task left. Why don't I have to complete number five, *Image?*"

"You will find the answer soon enough, Artemis. Our work here is complete, so we will leave any future decisions for the Duo Supreme Deities." Artemis watched as they turned and disappeared behind a narrow opening in the wall.

"Duo Supreme Deities? Who are they?" Artemis, bewildered, was beginning to lose his happy feeling and hope of leaving fairy capture. "You mean I have more fairy leaders to meet?" He worried there would be more tasks to complete, too. *When will this ordeal end?*

A bright light illuminated in front of him, nearly blinding him as he looked away and shielded his eyes. He closed his mouth slowly and waited as the light subsided. Two luminescent, regal-looking fairies stood still before him. They very slowly extended their arms outward toward him.

"Artemis," the deities spoke as one, "we are here to explain the final portion of your journey." The two glowed brightly as they continued on. "The atonement task list. Take it out of your pocket and review it again."

Artemis followed instructions only too willingly, unfolding the list nervously and watching the fifth atonement task letters begin to glow.

Artemis's bushy eyebrows rose high on his forehead, his eyes open wide. "I see the fifth task, and now the word is highlighted in bright glowing letters," Artemis answered, his hands shaking slightly as he held the crumpled paper. "It still says the word *Image,* but I'm not sure what to do about this—is it my image I have to work on? Is it Evelyn's or Reed's? Whose image am I supposed to atone for?"

"That's partly why we are here," the male deity replied in a deep voice.

The female deity continued, "Artemis, we want you to tell us how your image has been changed as you completed all the atonement tasks. As you think about that, look at your list with renewed insight."

Artemis saw his image as he looked toward the brilliant reflection before him; however, when he expected to see a mass of gray with a slightly hunched back and furrowed, bushy eyebrows defining his dark eyes, he saw nothing of the sort. He stood in front of the Duo Supreme Deities and saw beauty reflected back—his. He looked behind him to see who else might have been standing with him, but there was no one else. He could barely believe what he saw. The reflection was the same pixie he had known for years, but his appearance had changed considerably. He saw in the brilliant mirror before him a former pixie who stood taller and straighter than he'd ever remembered; he stretched his arm out to examine his wings, enlarged and sparkling in the light, caressing the new appearance.

"What color is this?" he asked. He struggled to find an accurate way to describe his new wings. They were no longer dark and cumbersome with heavy, jagged edges but a light translucent bluish hue with gold highlights catching the light as they waved.

"I had no idea my wings had changed so much." He turned away from his reflection and stroked his cheeks with his hands. "And my face . . . I'm beautiful. Well, at least I'm not at all homely or unattractive, and now it looks like my outside matches what I feel like on the inside."

Out of habit, he put his hands in his pocket where he usually pulled out the list of atonement tasks. He was so entranced with his new appearance, he had forgotten he'd already set the list on the table before him. Stepping closer to the table, he reread each line of the paper systematically and then shared his observation with the Duo Supreme Deities.

"I'm supposed to look at this list carefully," he said, repeating the directions aloud to himself. Rereading them countless times became a little frustrating, as nothing that he could see was different on the list . . . until he looked quickly from the top to the bottom. When he read the first letter of each task spelled out horizontally, it created a new word.

With a little uncertainty, Artemis said, "Well, I've searched the list, and I think I do see something. By completing all the tasks, something new is revealed both in the list and in myself." Artemis paused and looked at the list again. He read the first letter of each task from top to bottom. "Yes, I see it! I see the word that I didn't notice before; it spells *dignity*." Artemis grew excited and rather proud that he had figured it out largely on his own. He had heard the word before but wasn't completely sure what it meant.

The Duo Supreme Deities smiled, and one signaled to the squirrel guard to read aloud a proclamation.

"Artemis, we hereby anoint you to be a full-fledged elfin whose dignity–" The squirrel looked up from the scroll and leaned toward Artemis. "That means your sense of pride or your self-respect." Standing upright, the squirrel continued, "Whose dignity shall be evident in the brightness you live and lead with. From this day forward, you will be given all the rights of an elfin, and no longer will you be that of a pixie." The squirrel rolled up his scroll, tucked it in a container belted to his body, gave a respectful nod to the deities, and scurried to the exit door.

Artemis watched the squirrel scamper away while he digested his new title. *I'm not a pixie?* While he wasn't certain how he felt about that, he did know elfins were more highly regarded than pixies, were less apt to partake in mischief, and had more delicate features.

"I do feel like I've got so much more than I had as a pixie," Artemis said with a heightened sense of understanding. "I think I'll like being an elfin, and I *am* finished with the atonement list. Is that correct?" He stood up straight.

"Yes, Artemis, we believe as you studied your list, you saw how you changed by completing the tasks. As a result, your inward state has transformed your outward state over time, and we believe you are satisfied with the results."

"Am I? My dream has come true! I now look more like a true fairy." Artemis strutted around like a peacock. He knew very well that he would never reach the full beauty of a fairy, and that was very much all right with him. The improvement he saw in his appearance was remarkable.

Reality, however, began to suddenly set in, and Artemis felt forced to inquire in spite of not wanting to face the answer. "Just how long will this transformation last?"

"That will depend on you. You will be free to leave now to go your own way, but you will be required to go through an exit process to finalize your freedom tomorrow. Use your atonement task list. It will have been transformed just as you have." The Duo Supreme Deities slipped away after a quick flash of brightness.

Finally, the light at the end of the tunnel, Artemis thought. He was only too happy to do anything the fairy leaders requested. Leaving through the nearest exit, he was escorted by the bailiff finch down several flights to the bottom of the oak tree. Several insects working on a variety of paper tasks occupied the right portion of the room, and a couple of centipedes filed papers next to them as two heavily armored beetles stood on either side of the entrance with weapons in hand. Artemis was escorted to the counter directly in front of them, where a short line of small creatures were being processed. A plump, blind vole, just ahead of Artemis in line, was being helped by two grasshopper guides, one on either side of him, to sign his papers. Once he was processed and guided out of the room, it was Artemis's turn.

After about an hour of paperwork and instructions, Artemis was given the exit information. He was escorted out of the oak tree, and then he stood alone in the crisp, cold air. A sentinel crow flew overhead, cawing loudly to alert Artemis that he was still being watched constantly.

Artemis didn't mind that nor the frost that covered the grass and frozen ground. The sun, low in the autumn sky, shone on his face, and he soaked in its warmth as he gazed around and smelled the freshest air that he could remember. The autumn colors, in spite of losing their seasonal brilliance, looked more vivid than ever before to Artemis, and his newfound freedom helped make life taste and smell better than ever.

13.

A New Life

Artemis took the long route to Evelyn and Reed's home, savoring every aspect of liberation that he could soak in, and joy filled his heart as it never had before, causing a smile to reach from ear to ear. He found Evelyn and Reed in the kitchen preparing their typical after-school snacks and putting their schoolbags aside to complete homework.

"Surprise!" Artemis flew front and center onto the counter to announce his arrival; he could hardly wait to share his good news with the kids. Twirling around and beaming proudly, he asked, "Do you notice anything different about me?"

Evelyn and Reed stopped what they were doing and looked up to see Artemis strutting around.

"Oh, hey there, Artemis," Reed said as he swallowed the last bites of his banana.

Evelyn chimed in, "Hi, Artemis. You're looking quite dashing, I might say. In fact, I don't think you've ever looked quite this good! I love the new color your wings have taken on, and they do look way sturdier than they used to. Don't you agree, Reed?"

"Totally. And it almost looks like you've grown since you left us, Artemis." Reed put his hand to his hip. "Yep, I'd say you're looking handsomer each time we see you, but we've always considered how you look a uniqueness that helps make you special."

Evelyn adjusted her seat to get more comfortable. "We're very anxious to hear what you found out from the Fairy Council."

"Lots! The Fairy Council does, indeed, consider the atonement tasks complete, and so do the Duo Supreme Deities," he explained proudly.

"That's wonderful, Artemis!" Evelyn and Reed agreed.

"Wait a minute. You mean you met more fairies who are even higher up than Ashkin or the Fairy Council?" Reed was on the edge of his seat.

"Yes, and do you know what else I discovered—all on my own, I might add?" Pulling out the very wrinkled list from his pocket, Artemis held it out to the children. "Look at the atonement list again. You can make out the original task list; it's sort of faded into the background. Then look at the first letter of each word, and tell me what word it spells," he said, as if he had solved the world's most perplexing puzzle.

Reed pulled out the magnifying glass, and the kids studied the list. In mere moments, it was apparent.

"*Dignity!*" Reed exclaimed.

"You've got the answer, Reed!" Artemis's enthusiasm about his newfound understanding was clear. "The Fairy Council told me to read the atonement task list very carefully. Well, I can't tell you how many times I read and reread that list. I had already read it probably a hundred times, but then I read it very slowly, the way that they asked me to, and from a different viewpoint. Well, I turned the list around, upside down, and then I saw it, but the fifth task on the list is the one that stumped me."

Reed adjusted scattered homework on the kitchen counter to give Artemis a little more space. "Remind us what task was on your list, Artemis."

"The fifth task listed the word *Image*. Remember? When I looked at the Duo Supreme Deities—they're pretty important, you know—there was an incredibly bright light radiating from them; I could see my reflection when I looked at them, and I could see the outward changes that, I guess, my inside made. What did you call it again? My heart? Oh yeah, that's it. I guess my heart, and maybe even my head, changed the way I look on the outside. And now–don't get up. I'm considered an elfin!" Artemis announced proudly.

"An elfin? I've never heard of that. What is it?" Reed asked, moving in a little closer to look at Artemis from different angles. "Is that a good thing?"

"It's not bad, and it's certainly an improvement over what a pixie is. I'll have full use of my magical powers just as long as I continue to use them to help others, and elfins have the ability to move higher up on the fairy ladder of importance, but that'll take a while. That's okay, though. I'll keep at it, and I'll keep my new-and-improved appearance just as long as I keep trying to think about others first–oh, and I'm supposed to keep working on keeping my chin up. I think I can do that; I'll just take one day at a time. Wouldn't you agree that I look more like a fairy now?"

Before the kids could reply, their mother entered the kitchen, having just arrived home.

"Who were you two talking to?" she asked with her arm full of groceries. "I thought I heard a familiar voice." Mrs. Gunderson set her purse and bags down. When Evelyn glanced back at Artemis, she saw he had instantly vanished.

"Oh, hi, Mom. Uh . . . no, that was just Reed and me talking about school today. You might've heard one of us imitating our friends." Evelyn had gotten good at creating excuses by now.

"How was your day, Evelyn? Reed?"

As Mrs. Gunderson went to the cupboard, reached for a glass, and poured herself water, the kids watched Artemis quickly fly from behind a vase of flowers to an out-of-sight location on the top of the refrigerator. He was waiting for a safe moment to reappear.

"Well, who'll tell me about their day first?" Mrs. Gunderson asked, sitting down on a counter chair.

"Can it wait for dinnertime?" Evelyn asked, rummaging through her backpack. "I'd like to tackle these math problems while the lessons are fresh in my head."

"Yeah, and I wanna hurry and finish my snack so I can play with my space glider," Reed added.

Mrs. Gunderson suspiciously replied, "Okay, I suppose," and left to go upstairs. "I'll be right back to put those groceries away."

Artemis flew back down to the kids to continue their conversation. "Your mom sure looks like a nice lady."

Knowing her mother would return soon, Evelyn quickly moved the conversation along. "So now what? The atonement tasks were competed, and we understand how that was a way for you to work on your inward image, which caused your outward image to change."

"And watch this!" Artemis waved his hands in his typical magical movement, breaking the glass of water that Mrs. Gunderson had left on the counter.

The kids gasped, but before they could say anything, Artemis waved his hands again to reveal the glass whole again with the water inside, demonstrating his fully reacquired magical powers.

Impressed, Reed clapped.

Evelyn was more interested in understanding how the new Artemis came to be. "So did the fairy leaders fill you in about the calamities that happened with Reed's science experiment and the anniversary cake with the ambrosia? Did you get any credit for not getting revenge on Narcena?"

Artemis leaned in as if to share some juicy gossip. "I'm glad you asked! It turns out that those calamities, as you called them, were not caused by Narcena, because she never existed in the first place." Artemis caught the sound of his voice rising with residual anger but quickly quieted down.

"That's what our fairy friends explained to us recently." Evelyn looked at Reed for confirmation.

Nodding, Reed added, "We weren't sure what you knew up until now. In fact, we just learned about the real Narcena yesterday."

"And we found out why the fairies tested you like they did. I really didn't think it was the way the fairies typically operated," Evelyn continued.

"Well, part of me was very angry that they tricked me like that, and part of me understood that it actually helped me become stronger," said Artemis. "I guess it's kind of how your parents might teach you a lesson—doing something that is not their first choice of action, but what they think is the best decision. The fairy leaders used Narcena to test me to see how I'd react to the huge problems that Narcena—er, I mean, the fairies—caused, and since I had remained composed and didn't attempt to be hurtful in return, I passed their test with flying colors. I showed them that I was worthy of being free."

"I was pretty sure you'd come out of it all without too much trouble!" exclaimed Reed.

"We were surprised when we heard the fairies' explanation. I guess they knew what they were doing, and we can see in the end how it actually helped you, Artemis."

"The fairies *do* make life more beautiful." Artemis explained. "We know that fairies work to do great things for nature. But it was the fairy leaders who were strong enough to go against what they believed in to help strengthen and teach me." *Wow!* Artemis thought to himself. *I really have changed! Here I am, again standing up for someone who did something against me–or at least made life temporarily more difficult.* "They had faith that I could pull through both the muffin and ambrosia situations, and they were fully ready to step in if any situation got too out of hand, or if I fell short. I think that the fairy leaders saw promise in me that even I was never aware of."

Although Evelyn wanted to digest this information a bit more, she knew she needed to be hasty to find out more about the conversation Artemis had started before their mother came back to the kitchen. "All right, so the atonement tasks are considered completed. What's next for you?"

Before they could continue, Mrs. Gunderson returned, leaning her head into the kitchen while Artemis vanished quickly.

"I could swear that I heard you two talking to someone again. And what broke? I heard that accident all the way upstairs." She searched the kitchen floor and countertop for any remaining pieces of broken glass.

"I'm not sure what you're talking about, Mom," Reed answered innocently.

Mrs. Gunderson peered into the trash bin, sure she would see a deposit of broken glass, but not a bit was found. "Hmm, that's odd. I was certain that I heard a glass shatter. Oh, well, it's been a long day. Maybe I'll lie down and rest before I help Evelyn with dinner." She quickly put away the few grocery items and returned to her bedroom, mumbling to herself.

* * *

After dinner, the kids returned to their rooms to complete homework, with Rupert tagging along behind as usual. Reed watched Rupert run up the stairs just after Evelyn rushed up, and he wondered if the dog followed them wherever they went because they were his food source or if it was simply for companionship. Maybe he, like Reed, always wanted to be part of the action. Regardless, each headed straight to their respective rooms to wait for Artemis's reappearance. They were eager to learn more about what would happen to him next on his journey as an elfin, and Rupert coiled up on the floor near Evelyn's feet.

"Hey, Evelyn." Reed popped his head into her room. "Did Artemis show up yet?"

"Not yet." Evelyn stood from her desk and walked toward Reed. "I think I understand what he was telling us about what he went through and how it changed him for the better, but now that he has changed, there's definitely no chance for him to go back to the pixies. I wonder where he's going to live."

"I've been wondering the same thing. I know he's been

worried about that for a while. We can be fairly sure the fairies wouldn't allow him to live among them in the pine forest, and we *know* the pixies wouldn't allow him to live with them!"

Evelyn nodded. Without warning other than a small bark from Rupert, Artemis flew down onto Reed's shoulder.

"What are you two up to?"

Rupert strained to get a good whiff of Artemis.

"Hi, Artemis," Reed said. "Evelyn and I were just chatting about where your new home will be now that you're an elfin. I know you can't go back to live with your old pixie friends."

"And I really wouldn't want to anymore. I've liked being here with you and Evelyn."

As the kids looked at each other, sharing the clear thought of having Artemis somehow live in their new home with the family, their mom startled them, appearing at the door, having listened to the entire conversation.

"I knew I heard an elfin voice!" she exclaimed.

Both children turned around in shock.

"Mom! Hi!" Startled, Evelyn hardly knew what to say. "We didn't know you were standing there." Evelyn looked at Reed as Artemis left in a flash to dart behind a book on the desk.

Rupert greeted Mrs. Gunderson by licking her ankle, as if giving her clearance to enter the room. "I clearly heard you two talking to an elfin or a pixie; I'd recognize their voices anywhere." She continued scanning Evelyn's room as she sat on the edge of the bed next to Reed.

Evelyn and Reed stared at each other, completely unsure how to respond. At this point, the two were tired of hiding their secret from their parents.

"You know, I haven't been able to tell you about pixies, elfins, or even fairies, because I knew even my own children might say something that would put them at risk." She moved to Evelyn's desk and faced the two kids. "It's time we had this talk."

Reed was quite surprised. "You mean about the birds and the bees?" He was horrified at the possibility of such a discussion, especially with Evelyn in the room.

"No, silly. That's for another day. I think it's time I tell you about a sensational event that has had an enormous impact on my life."

Somehow, Evelyn knew that her mom had connected the dots, as she so typically did. She wondered if she would have the same knack when she was a mother someday.

The kids gave their mother their full attention, as Mrs. Gunderson prepared to fill them in. Evelyn looked up to the edge of her dresser to see Artemis sitting next to the jewelry box, wanting to take in her story as well.

"Well, where should I begin?" Mrs. Gunderson said. "When I was about your age, I lived not far from the horse farm that we visited a short while back."

Evelyn suddenly recalled her mom telling her stories about life on the farm as a young girl. "Oh yeah, now I remember, Mom. You told me that years ago."

Mrs. Gunderson continued, "I learned about the fairies and pixies much the same way I think you probably stumbled upon them. I would visit the pine woods all the time by myself, which is where I learned about the fairies. Over time, it became more evident that the fairies and pixies were at war, so much so that the pixies had managed to start a fire that burned down the entire grove of pine woods. You can imagine how angry the fairies were at this. Ever since, the fairies have blamed the pixies for devastating their home. Naturally, the pixies say that if the fairies hadn't been involved in such a heated battle, the fire wouldn't have gotten out of hand."

Evelyn and Reed sat entranced.

"The oak tree in the corner of the pine grove survived the fire along with a couple of the pine trees near where the oak tree stood, but this patch of woods was largely destroyed by that fire," she asserted.

"Oh no! Were any of the fairies hurt?" Evelyn inquired.

"Most got out of their homes in time to be safe, but there were, if I remember correctly, two or three that got stuck in the burning brush and didn't make it out in time. That's when the pixies tried their best to steer clear of the fairies and why the fairies rule the forest. It's also part of the reason the pixies are jealous of the fairies. You see, the Duo Supreme Deities decided to punish the pixies for the fire for eternity by making the fairies more beautiful and powerful than the pixies."

Reed interjected, "Yeah, we heard about the fairy deities!"

Rupert sat at the bottom of Mrs. Gunderson's feet as if he, too, were listening to her story.

She continued, "One of the fairies even befriended me after she saw me visit the place of the fire time and time again." She smiled at the thought of the friendship she'd developed with that particular fairy. "Over time, she trusted me enough to tell me the whole story. In fact, she still visits me regularly, but I've always promised not to reveal her secrets. And a while after I became friends with the fairy, a couple of pixies from the horse farm started showing up at my house. Apparently, they somehow learned I had become friends with the fairy."

Surprised, Evelyn asked, "What did the pixies do when

they heard about you and the fairy?"

"Ohhh, they were very rotten. They caused so many headaches around our house. At first, we simply thought strange little things were happening—like the clock telling the wrong time, the television reception messing up, and the garage door opening and closing mysteriously. You know, the problems started innocently, but then they got bigger. I remember the entire garden we planted one year was covered in frost that ruined all the vegetables and flowers."

"Why would you think that a pixie was the cause of garden frost?" Reed asked.

"In the middle of a sweltering summer in July? Only the garden had frost on it—none of the other trees or plants in the area were affected." Mrs. Gunderson went on, "Well, it got worse around the house, and the fairies didn't like it, nor did we. The pixies began fighting with the fairies near the pine woods, but then their fights would move to this area or to that one. There'd be battles near the pines, in the farmers' crops, and in the horses' pastures. I remember one of them got pretty nasty. The Eddy family had a stable of horses near their barn, and Farmer Eddy would ride his horse to survey his crops daily. Unfortunately, he became the innocent victim of a fight that broke out between the fairies and the pixies."

A Pixie's Transformation

Mrs. Gunderson's face became sterner, and the wrinkles on her forehead grew prominent. She continued, "The pixies' fighting startled Farmer Eddy's horse so badly that he was bucked off, and the horse unfortunately landed on the poor man's legs!" She took a deep breath and paused. "He never walked again." She shook her head and sighed. "The pixies immediately regretted their actions so much that they urged the horses to use Farmer Eddy's wagon filled with hay to bring him back to his house, where he could get help. He had a lot of farmland that needed tending to, and he had a number of farm animals that needed attention. The pixies knew if they didn't help the farmer, the fairies' punishment would be unthinkable. Fortunately, because the pixies all worked together that summer using their magic to help the farmer out, the fairies didn't punish them as severely. In the end, the pixies continued to envy the fairies, but the Duo Supreme Deities . . . You said you heard about them, right?"

Reed answered, "Yes, our elfin friend, Artemis, told us about them. They're like the supreme fairy gods, I think."

"A long time ago, the Duo Supreme Deities were only in charge of the fairies. After the farmer's accident, the pixies lost the ability to govern themselves. The pixie gods, Aure and Gaia, were cast out of power by the fairies and made to work alongside the rest of the pixies."

"The pixies sound evil," Evelyn said as she looked up at Artemis.

Mrs. Gunderson continued, "The pixies were always jealous of the fairies. They didn't realize that their mischievous actions would only lead to unhappiness for themselves and others. Also, the accident eliminated any chance for the pixies to have access to the pine woods."

Evelyn wondered aloud, "What happened to the fairies who befriended you?"

"They returned to the pine forest once the forest regrew, and the pixies returned to their homes near the horse farm–with the exception, I think, of about half a dozen who had to atone for the fire. You can probably guess that not all the pixies completed their atonements. They were found guilty and had to live in the Perpetual Sealand of Indemnity, except for one female pixie. Because she was the only one who was successful with her atonements, she earned the right to be an elfin." Mrs. Gunderson stood up from the chair. "Now seems to be the right time to tell you kids the rest of the story."

Thoroughly enthralled, Evelyn had to ask, "There's more to the story?"

Reed picked up Rupert as he said, "You mean it doesn't end there? Wow, Mom! This story is as good as most of the movies I've seen." Reed shifted to get comfortable, with Rupert on his lap.

Artemis stretched after listening in fascination. He had been away at training camp as a young pixie when many of these events took place. He had heard only the pixie version of the story, which, naturally, left out many facts. He was finally compelled to speak up. Mustering all his courage, he said, "Uh, hello there, mother of the house."

Mrs. Gunderson walked up to Artemis, who was now standing with his hands crossed behind his back. He walked backward slowly, waiting for what she was going to say now that she saw him in the room.

"Are you the one my children call Artemis?"

"Yes, ma'am," he said nervously.

"Hello, Artemis. I see you've gone through somewhat of a transformation, too."

"How do you know that?"

"Well, you don't look like a typical pixie. Your wings look a little more like a fairies' do. If you look like that, well, I know you wouldn't be able to live with the pixies anymore. Did you have to atone for any of the pranks you and the other pixies pulled?"

"Yes, ma'am, and I can say those atonements are some of my finer moments," Artemis answered proudly and stuck his chest out.

"Yes, you do look a lot like someone I know. Someone

very small but incredibly mighty, and I love her dearly. She's been a lifelong friend to me, and frankly, I don't know what I would've done without her. She's helped me through many tough moments in my life, and she's worked hard to stay out of the dreaded PSI."

Reed liked that his mother was aware of their interactions with the fairies and pixies and that he and Evelyn no longer had to keep secrets from their parents.

"It was my understanding that because this tiny friend of mine was least involved with the farmer's accident, she showed the most promise to be rehabilitated." Mrs. Gunderson first looked at Evelyn, then to Reed, and again to Artemis. "I suppose you kids are ready to know." Her long hesitation made the kids a little nervous at what she might be announcing. After what seemed like several minutes, she finally blurted out, "There's been a pixie who has always lived with us, and like Artemis here, she was able to become and remain an elfin."

Reed interrupted excitedly, "You mean we have our own pixie–I mean, elfin–that lives with us? Here? Where is she? Can I see her?"

"She's stayed confined and comfortable so that she wasn't discovered by you two."

Artemis was very intrigued. "Are you saying that there's always been an elfin who lives here with you? Can

I meet her, too?"

Mrs. Gunderson walked toward Evelyn's bedroom door. "I don't see why not." As she was about to leave, she said to Artemis, "And I'm looking forward to hearing, in the near future, how you ended up here with my children."

Reed looked at Artemis and then at Evelyn. He chuckled and said, "It's a long story, Mom, but we'd be happy to tell you all about it."

"Wait here," Mrs. Gunderson directed. "I'll be back in a jiffy."

The immense excitement and anticipation the three felt at that moment left them giggling and squirming as they waited for Mrs. Gunderson to return.

Mrs. Gunderson cautiously entered the room where waiting eyes hoped to capture a view of their new friend. As she carefully brought her hands from behind her back to be cupped in front of her, she presented the surprise houseguest, "Let me introduce to you, Clio. Clio, this is my daughter, Evelyn and my son, Reed."

Clio giggled shyly, adding in a demure and high voice, "I already know who everyone is." She paused. "I've watched both of you kids grow up."

Reed wasn't so sure what to think of that statement.

With a most serious expression, Mrs. Gunderson interjected a warning as she continued holding Clio in her hand. "Remember, this still remains *our* news, and we cannot breathe a word of it to anyone! Clio has made a small area in our bedroom closet into her home because she couldn't live with the pixies any longer." Three pairs of eyes stared intently at the tiny handheld elfin. "She worked hard to change her troublesome behavior and build a trusting relationship with me, and because she helped me, she became stronger, more confident, and more charming. I suppose it's similar to what you've had to go through you, Artemis, though I'm sure you'll have to talk with her more sometime and compare your journeys. What I am certain about is that she'll find it exciting to meet someone who looks like her."

It seemed like the perfect opportunity for Artemis to inquire about his future living arrangements.

"Do you suppose I can find a home here, too?" he asked meekly as he looked into the eyes of each family member. It seemed that an eternity passed before he heard a reply.

Reed was the first to respond. "Please, Mom. We love Artemis, and he's been very good to us while he made his atonements."

Evelyn added, "We'd do our best to make sure that he follows the house rules."

"I think Clio should get to know Artemis first and see if they can live in the same place. Then it'll definitely be on a trial basis before your dad and I can give you a final answer."

Evelyn and Reed looked at each other and smiled broadly.

"That's fine with us," Evelyn said as she took Artemis, who was shaking like a leaf, into her hand. "Well, let me *officially* introduce you to Clio."

Artemis looked over his shoulder, finding it hard to face his new elfin friend until he got a thumbs-up from Evelyn. Artemis obviously wanted to make a good impression on Clio, and he wasn't certain of whether he was feeling more thankful or relieved to have someone nearby who was similar to himself and to whom he could relate. He started to flutter and sputter in excitement, buzzing from side to side and performing loop-de-loops. Evelyn and Reed's eyes tried to follow him for a while, but they soon gave up and simply looked at each other. Artemis flew around as quickly as an angry hornet kicked out of its nest.

Evelyn had to slow the zipping elfin way down. "Artemis! Get a hold of yourself and calm down!"

With a halting landing, Artemis settled back onto the dresser, where he stood panting heavily as he faced where Mrs. Gunderson held Clio. Artemis held his breath while Evelyn and Reed stood watching Artemis gain his composure. Trying to sound rather official, Evelyn announced, "Clio, may I introduce to you our friend, Artemis."

Artemis snapped his fingers quickly to create a colorful mound in his hand, wanting to leave nothing to chance. Reed's eye caught the appearance of a small floral bouquet that Artemis pulled out. *Perhaps this will help Clio's impression of me,* he thought.

Mrs. Gunderson smiled broadly. "Awwww. That's so lovely, Artemis."

She continued, sounding a little guarded, "Clio has a very special place in my heart." Artemis's gaze became fixated on Clio as he presented her with the flowers.

"Thank you, Artemis," Clio shyly responded as she smelled the bouquet and smiled.

"Hel–hel–uh, hello, Clio. It's so exciting to meet you." Artemis couldn't think what else to say as he got an up close and personal view of Clio. To him, she was stunning.

Evelyn noticed the petite elfin wore some of her old Barbie doll's clothes. Clio's shoulder-length hair was combed neatly, something both male and female pixies rarely bothered with, and her hair was not a dull, mossy hue; it held a brighter color, like sunshine. Although Clio was not as lean as most fairies, she was not as plump as a typical pixie either. She smiled broadly when her eyes met Artemis's, as she she, too, was eager to get acquainted with someone who looked like herself. It had been a very long time since she'd had such a companion to talk to.

Her voice was sweet music to Artemis, who had not heard a female elfin speak before. He wanted to quickly think of another question to ask so he could hear her talk more. While he thought, he noticed that her wings also had a more solid look with a brighter color to match the rest of her body. The Gundersons simply stared at the two while listening intently to their conversation.

"So, Clio. What do you think of the family dog?" Artemis smacked his forehead as he immediately wondered why he had asked *that* question. Before she could answer, Artemis inquired, "I mean, have you met the Gundersons' dog?" What was he thinking? Of course she'd already met Rupert. He was getting more embarrassed with every word.

Reed saw Artemis's nervousness and stepped in. "Clio, I think Artemis simply wants to know how you get along with Rupert. Why don't you start from the beginning, Artemis, and ask her how long she's been here?"

"Yeah, you're right. I'm just so nervous, and I've got a bunch of questions running through my head. How long have you been here, Clio, and how did you get here in the first place?" Artemis wasn't sure where to even start with all the questions swimming through his mind.

Clio looked shyly to Mrs. Gunderson as if to get permission to give the information.

Mrs. Gunderson smiled broadly. "Go ahead, Clio. It's
all right. I knew this would come out someday, but I hadn't
anticipated another elfin being part of the picture."

Smiling to her captive audience, Clio explained, "You
see, when the pine forest burned down, a few fairies and
pixies had to find new homes. While I wasn't living in the
forest, I lived close enough for my home to be destroyed.
My family died in the home, too." Clio paused, bowing her
head in sadness.

"Oh, I'm sorry to hear that, Clio." Evelyn was the first
to extend her condolences.

"Me, too," Reed chimed in, who then looked at Artemis, who was sitting on the dresser and resting on his
hands as he listened.

"Oh," Artemis said sadly. He quickly got Reed's hint.
"Me, too." Besides his appearance, he knew he had another way to connect with Clio. "I mean, I'm very sorry that
you lost your family. I lost mine, too, but that was when
I was a really young pixie. I *do* understand your feelings."
Artemis saw a hint off appreciation in Clio's eyes as she
continued with her story. He felt his heart warm, which
made him think again how giving affection—even if just

through words—was sort of like getting the same affection in return. He planned on giving and getting more of it in the future.

Clio continued, "Thank you. After I lost my family, I was too upset to take part in any pixie mischief. I remember being so sad that all I wanted to do was find a new home and cry and cry and cry some more. That's when Mrs. Gunderson found me in a stick home near the tall grasses just a short distance from the forest. I was so caught up in my sadness that I didn't care if I was found. I didn't even noticed that there was a girl–Mrs. G.–walking nearby." Clio looked up to Mrs. Gunderson and they shared a look of mutual admiration. "When she discovered me, she picked me up and took me to her home. I had reached such a point of desperation that I didn't care what happened to me."

Mrs. Gunderson interjected, "When I found Clio, she was extremely brokenhearted. I was about your age when I found her, and I didn't tell a single person–especially after I learned how much she had been through. She was grateful that I had no intentions of hurting her, and we developed a friendship from there. I became her family, guiding her and helping her in any way that I could, and I think Clio was so grateful to have someone to love and help her, she didn't want to return to the naughty pixie lifestyle."

"I suppose she found herself changing physically like Artemis the more she made positive choices in her life," Evelyn said, noting how similar Clio looked to the transformed Artemis.

"Mom, now that Artemis and Clio have talked, do you think Artemis can live in our house with Clio?" Reed asked excitedly at the prospect.

Mrs. Gunderson looked directly at Artemis. "I won't have a problem with that as long as he follows the house rules. We'll have to give Clio a chance to get to know Artemis, of course. I'm sure the same fairies have made him well aware of what would happen if he ever returned to his old ways. If Clio would welcome him, I would also. In fact, I think Clio could show him the ropes around here and help him learn the expectations in our household."

"I'd be happy to," Clio's tiny voice sweetly said, smiling and not being able to take her eyes off her new friend.

"Really? I can stay here?" Artemis asked. "Oh, boy, life is grand." Artemis flung his arms open and smiled with a sense of joy and comfort completely new to him. Taking Clio's hand, he said, "I know that my life can be a happy one by being part of a family. I will do my best to help you all because . . ." Artemis looked at Reed and Evelyn with an enormous smile. "Because I've come to know love and how to be grateful."

Artemis saw several smiles, as Mr. Gunderson walked in with a laundry basket of Evelyn's clean, folded clothes.

"Here you all are," he said. "I've been busy with the laundry downstairs, and you're busy chatting away. What's the powwow about?"

Mrs. Gunderson put her arm on Mr. Gunderson's shoulder. "Well, dear, it seems that our family has expanded."

"You're kidding, right? What are you talking about?"

"It seems the kids have had a run-in with a little friend, just like I did a long time ago. Meet Artemis." She directed Mr. Gunderson's view to the small elfin who now stood next to Clio on the desk.

"Well, it's nice to meet you, Artemis. I look forward to hearing all about how you ended up here. I do hope you'll get along well with our sweet Clio. Oh, I almost forgot. Evelyn, you've got to remember to check your pockets before putting your clothes in the laundry basket. I almost washed your pants with this picture in the pocket."

At first, Evelyn wasn't sure what her father was referring to. Then she reached over to take the picture from him. Of course! How could she be so forgetful about something so important to the fairies and to Reed? And she'd done precisely what she had been warning Reed not to do with the picture! It was too easy to get distracted and forget its whereabouts.

Reed caught sight of the photograph that his dad handed over. "Ohhh, that was the photo I took of the fairies. I thought you got rid of that a while ago, Evvie."

"That must mean that you've had a lot on your mind, Ev," Mrs. Gunderson said as she put her arms around Evelyn's shoulders. "I know that the busier I get and the more I have to think about, the more I forget, but now we have a couple of tiny beings around here who can help with us with things like that. I'll take this picture, as I know some other tiny friends who will want to witness its destruction."

Reed's eyes followed the picture as Evelyn handed it to their mother, and although he still wanted to keep it for himself, he understood the fairies' position. Besides, he'd have his own family of elfins in the house to see with his own eyes.

Mrs. Gunderson smiled and left with Mr. Gunderson as the two discussed the small addition to their family. Rupert slept on the floor as an intense but fair discussion ensued between Evelyn and Reed about how their time and responsibilities would be equally shared among Artemis and Clio—and of course Rupert.

While the family got busy making arrangements, Clio took Artemis around the house to familiarize him with the routines and how they fit in with the family's expectations. As he flew around the home, Artemis smiled broadly and let out a huge sigh of contentment at the new chapter about to begin.

About the Author

After growing up in a suburb of St. Paul, Minnesota, Faith Eilertson now resides in Wisconsin, where she retired early after twenty years as an elementary school teacher due to MS. She next pursued a degree from culinary school, where she put her skills to work as a caterer and pastry chef. The story of Artemis had been "stewing" inside her head for years before she put it down on paper to provide readers an enjoyable experience and bring a smile to their faces. If she isn't baking a favorite recipe, Faith can be found spending time with her family and three French bulldogs—all of whom bring her countless daily smiles.

About the Illustrator

Kari Vick lives along the north shore of Lake Superior in Lutsen, Minnesota. For over thirty years her career took her from the high arctic to the northwest coast, in search of the art of distant lands. Family adventures, from the Himalaya Mountains to the fjords of Norway, have introduced her to enchanted beings around the world. She now works full time as an artist and has illustrated nine books. Whether working in her studio or garden, she listens for stories told by ravens and mushrooms and captures them in her paintings. To see more of her work, visit www.karivick.com.